Elvis's imaginative writing style creates a page-turner with plenty of surprises. The story is well paced, full of endearing characters, and you can't wait to see what happens next!

- Kathi Masters

Elvis's steady flow of vivid images and solid storyline will captivate and entertain readers of all ages.

- Dereck Fisher, Audiovisual Specialist.

I read this book and was absolutely in awe! The author of this book brings so much color and fantasy to anyone who reads it. I read this book to my three younger children every night, and they could not wait for the next evening for more pages to be read to them.

- Kathryn Steffen- ALOM

Once Upon a Childhood

Shelly,

Thanks for all your help!!!

w/ Love,

Eliz Ray

THE WINDHEART CHRONICLES

Once Upon a Childhood

ELVIS RAY

TATE PUBLISHING *& Enterprises*

Published by Tate Publishing & Enterprises, LLC
127 E. Trade Center Terrace | Mustang, Oklahoma 73064 USA
1.888.361.9473 | www.tatepublishing.com

Tate Publishing is committed to excellence in the publishing industry. The company reflects the philosophy established by the founders, based on Psalm 68:11,
"The Lord gave the word and great was the company of those who published it."

Book design copyright © 2007 by Tate Publishing, LLC. All rights reserved.
Cover design by Brandon Wood
Interior design by Steven Jeffrey

Published in the United States of America

ISBN: 978-1-60462-107-5

1. Juvenile Fiction   2. Fantasy
07.09.12

ACKNOWLEDGMENTS:

I would first like to thank my Heavenly Father who created us with the ability to dream, in every sense of the word.

I thank my parents for their love and support.

I thank my sister, Sonja, who was my first audience, and editor.

I also thank my younger brother, Rodney, who always provided me with feed back throughout the writing process.

Last, but far from least, I would like to thank my readers.

Without you to read them, my words have no value.

Contents

PROLOGUE

Long before the light had been granted the power to push darkness into night, the world which held no name was torn by war. The war was senseless. Even though the world was so vast that it seemed to hold no borders, like many other wars it was a battle for land that the various creatures waged. Even though the sea, landscape, and sky appeared to go on forever...it was as if the creatures only held interest in land if it was already the property of another. It was a dark time in every sense of the phrase. Dragons rained destruction from the skies, while trolls and ogres crushed all in their path. Chaotic Chimeras unleashed waves of disaster wherever they trod, and sea serpents devoured any who dared to come too close to their watery domains. Even among these frightening monsters, one conqueror was unquestionably the deadliest. He was a human by the name of William. William belonged to the clan of the West Wind. Not even the ancient dragons were fools enough to stand in his way.

William had learned sword techniques from his father, and used them to create his own sword style. His most revered technique was his blade of shadows. It focused all the darkness in the area into his sword, Shadow Gale. One stroke of his blade could destroy all things within a radius of up to five miles around him.

Once William had claimed enough land, he established a kingdom for himself. It is not in human nature to destroy so many lives and bare no scars on the conscience. William showed no remorse for his actions, but that was only because he was much disciplined when it came to hiding his feelings. His dreams, during sleep or waking, dragged him off to battle fields where he was forced to witness the horrible crimes he had committed against creation.

One evening William left his castle and went for a walk around his kingdom. When he stopped to draw a drink from a well, he met a beautiful woman…her name was Shauna. In time they fell deeply in love. In two years more Shauna gave him a son who they decided to name Edward, after his own father. It was only with his family that he was able to feel any semblance of peace. In fact, it was only with his family that he was able to feel at all.

For the first time in William's life, he could say that he was truly happy. Not even the occasional onslaughts against his kingdom bothered him much. His skill was as lethal as ever, and attacks were few. Just when he was beginning to accept this feeling of contentment, a horrible plague tore through his land like a black hurricane. The disease claimed the lives of those in his kingdom, his castle, and his family. William was the only one to survive, but he refused to live without them. He did not leave the side of his then-silent wife and child...not even to eat or drink. He began to pass from the world slowly, consumed by his grief. Before he died, as he clung to the bodies of the only ones who had given him peace, in his frailty he made a wish and cast it into the darkness. He wished to end all existence, but not before others felt the pain he had come to know.

Even after the man died, the wish he made remained. It grew in power feeding on the dark memories that stained the land. It granted itself a name...a name to reflect its dark purpose to destroy all worlds. It called itself the Oblivion King. Drifting about the countryside, it found warriors on the brink of death. The Oblivion King would offer them the chance to live.

More often than not, the poor souls would accept. If the Oblivion King felt they looked strong enough he would use their bodies as his own. But, if they had less power than the body he was currently possessing, he would make them his servants and feed on the negative energy they generated while wreaking havoc. The monster grew in power at such a rate that no one knew how to stand up to him.

It was at the council of ancients that a royal family of fairies made a suggestion. The eldest fairy stood up and spoke, "It is my suggestion that we gather as many allies as possible to wage war against the dark king." There was much murmuring among those gathered.

Quietly a large centaur walked out from among his people. Looking around the chamber he raised his hands in question, "There are no allies strong enough. Perhaps the dragons...but they would have no interest in helping us. The dark king leaves them to their own devices…they have no quarrel with him."

The elder fairy smiled, "The dragons may change their point of view one day. But, I was thinking more along the lines of seeking help from the Great Storm. With the awesome power of the elements backing us, we may be able to at least seal away the dark one."

It was agreed. With the aid of the Great Storm they sealed the Oblivion King within a sphere of light. The dark one was sealed for countless years, until the tragic past that befell William's kingdom returned to repeat itself, as dark histories often do. Not only did his dark power overwhelm the barrier sealing him, but he changed its nature and made it into his fortress—crushing a beautiful kingdom in the process.

It seemed that the peaceful times had forever come to an end. The dark one's servants devastated the world's populace, while the Oblivion King himself continued to gain in power. During his campaigns the dark king heard of another world. He was told that his nemesis, the Storm of Legend, had been known to visit it for various periods of time. He also heard that this was the world which had come into existence slightly before his own, and that the two worlds were connected by an unbreakable bond. He would destroy that world as soon as he was finished with this one. Despite the hopeless situation, all was not lost. Destiny had already made a reply to the dark one's evil. The reply was likened to a flower of hope, a flower that was ready to bloom all at once…upon a childhood, that is.

Once Upon a Childhood

THE WINDHEARTS' SUMMER

Once upon a time...Hmmm, not quite right in this case. Once upon a childhood...Yes, let's go with that. Our story begins with an eleven year old girl by the name of Celest Windheart. Celest had two younger brothers. John, who was eight, acted much more grown up than he should. Perhaps this was due to the fact that he was born blind and took little for granted. Eric, the youngest, was nearly two years old. To him anything and everything was a toy to be bitten, thrown, and hidden.

The summer was hot and children were to be found everywhere, enjoying the warm breeze and playing with their friends. The Windhearts, on the other hand, found the company of each other more than adequate to pass the time. Early each morning Celest would go into her brothers' rooms and wake them up for another day of vacation. Together, they would watch early morning cartoons. Eric could not yet speak in full sentences, but none the less enjoyed leaping about the room while pretending to be a super hero and sputtering gibberish. For John, this summer morning ritual was more like story time at school… only much more enjoyable. If Celest saw something that she thought John would find interesting she would take care explaining whatever it happened to be in great detail. He also loved it when they watched the animal channel together. John was simply fascinated by the incredible variety of creatures that shared the planet with them.

One morning Celest walked into John's room earlier than she usually did. Thinking it might be fun to sneak up on him, she approached his bed as silently as a kitten would while preparing to pounce on an unsuspecting sibling. Celest smiled quietly as she stood next to his bed. When she looked down she saw John staring blankly at the ceiling. *Maybe he fell asleep with his eyes open last night?* she thought. Just as she was about to shake him awake John smiled, "Morning, Celest!"

Celest looked shocked, but only for a moment. "Morning…I just don't see why people are able to pick on you so easily. You always seem to know if anyone is around you. I wonder how you do it."

John shrugged and said, "Don't know. It's like I can sense their…feelings? But I can tell you why people tease me. Just because I know someone is there does not mean I can do anything about it."

Celest sighed, "I guess you're right. Let's go get Eric up."

Her youngest brother was also already up and had already began his super hero act. As she stepped into the room, Celest found a sharp piece of plastic from a now-destroyed toy truck waiting to greet her from beneath her bare feet. She received the greeting with a shout of pain.

Reaching down she picked up the remains of Eric's truck, "Scratch another one. You go through toys like crazy. What gets me is that you've broken toys that real trucks run over on TV just to show how they *can't* be broken!" Eric laughed out loud before bumping past her legs to get to the living room.

Celest helped to get her brothers fed before sitting down to eat herself. They watched TV and waited for their mom to get up. Mrs. Windheart was going to take them to church in just a little while. Celest was all for going; she loved everything she learned when she was there. Not to mention the fact that she loved spending time with her mom, who would often take them to the mall afterwards, just to stretch their legs. The only problem was how bored she sometimes got. When this happened, her imagination tended to take her off on wonderful adventures. If it was not an adventure, then she just pretended the world around her was a little more interesting.

Celest remembered a time when she was little, about three months before John arrived in the world. They were at church and she became so bored that she imagined the little flames on the candles were dancing for her. What an imagination she had! To her it really looked like the flames were dancing for her amusement. Once or twice Celest could have sworn that she saw a flame pirouette up off the candle. Mrs. Windheart looked from Celest's blank face to the candles at which she was staring. Celest looked at her mom and felt sorry that she had totally spaced off. She knew that they came to church for a good reason. Her mom cocked an eyebrow and turned her attention back to the front.

Celest was just toying with the possibility of little flames actually trying to entertain her when Mrs. Windheart came down the stairs with her usual good morning smile. Celest always felt a deep respect for her mother. Even though her dad only came around for short visits every few years, Mrs. Windheart always displayed a quiet strength and unending confidence. Celest did not think that there was anything on earth beyond her mother's capabilities.

At church they discussed how death entered into the world, and how mankind was sent a redeemer to provide us with a chance to escape it. Celest wondered what other evils could have been brought about by humankind's weaknesses and felt an unexplainable shiver down her spine.

After church they went to the mall and walked around for a while. As Mrs. Windheart bought the kids something to drink she asked Celest and John what they would like to do when they grew up. Celest told her mother that she wanted to be a doctor or a veterinarian. Mrs. Windheart smiled at her daughter's compassion. In her opinion it was one of Celest's best characteristics. John made everyone laugh by saying, "I don't know. But maybe I'll be a driving instructor or something—it should be exciting!" The summer continued to be an incredibly restful and pleasant time. The Windhearts wished that it would go on forever, but time waits for no man and soon the first day of the school year was upon them.

CELEST AND THE PORTAL

The first Monday of the school year was a little hectic…
perhaps more than *a little*. Getting breakfast, backpacks,
and school lunches ready in twenty minutes was no easy
task. Mrs. Windheart was going a little bananas looking
for her car keys, while Eric sat in the corner with a mon-
key-like gleam in his eyes. She was very relieved to find
her keys on top of the refrigerator. Not only had she found
them, but to make things better there was only a little
drool on them. Celest loved going to school, but hated the
way the other kids picked on John. She was very protective of her family members. Just the other year she had
to tell off a group of kids for hiding John's walking stick
from him.

After dropping Eric off at day care, Celest and John
were ready to be dropped off at their own school, Golden
River. The entire day up until 11:30 a.m. went great; John
and Celest both discovered that their new teachers were

really nice. The day, however, took a turn for the worst when lunch time came around.

Celest walked out onto the playground to see John getting hit in the back of his head with a rock. The boy who threw the rock was laughing, "He can't even see where it's coming from!" His laughter turned to fear as John's body fell into the gravel with a sick crunch. He was more frightened when he was lifted into the air by his shirt.

Celest was now staring into his face, "What have you done?" she growled. She was just about to let him have it when a teacher came out and told her to put the boy down. She was sent to detention while her brother was rushed to the hospital.

Celest was sitting in the empty detention room thinking about how unfair it was that her brother was hurt, and she was being punished for sticking up for him. Celest forgot about brooding when the hands on the clock began to spin backwards, that is, before the clock melted and slid off the wall into a puddle on the floor. Where the clock had been, a portal now sparkled gently. After a few moments had past, the part of the wall beneath the portal slid out in sections. The sections created a stairway leading up to the portal.

Young children are by nature very curious creatures, and Celest was no exception. Wanting a closer look she walked up the stairs to the portal. As she leaned closer, she was sucked into a tunnel made of light. Celest's eyes widened with fear and surprise, but soon her fear was replaced with intense wonder. At first, the colorful tunnel was like a gentle slide, much like the one out on her school's playground. Then it dropped off so sharply that if felt like she was falling off of a tall building. Next, the tunnel began to spiral and suddenly it felt as if she was flying straight into the air—perhaps she felt this way because she was.

Celest flew out the other side of the warp hole, and twenty-eight feet into the air. She thought she was dead meat as she fell back to the earth. Ready for the worst, she closed her eyes and waited for the crash, but it never came. The fall ended with her landing on something that felt like a huge velvet pillow stuffed with goose down. It was very surprising when the "pillow" whinnied as it slid her gently to the ground.

It was a very strange sight that greeted her when she finally stood up. A great gray stallion with wings as dark as his body loomed over her. Looking closer, he was gray not because of his fur, but because his body was made of swirling clouds. In a timid voice Celest asked, "Did you catch me?" The great beast whinnied again as it bowed its huge head. "I need to get home..." she said as she looked around. "Will you keep me company until I do?" The storm cloud steed nodded again as it dropped to its front knees allowing Celest to mount his back. She smiled as she asked her next question, "If it's not too corny, would it be okay if I called you 'Stormy'?" She took the boost in speed and the loud whinny to mean yes. The two flew well into the night, and even as she enjoyed the starlight, she couldn't help thinking about her family and if she would ever see them again. Suddenly, a large golden eagle rushed passed them. After a second, countless warm memories swelled within Celest's mind. "John!" she shouted as loud as she could over the wind.

The eagle circled back and landed on Stormy's head.

"Celest?" John asked happily. "So this is what you look like! Do you look like Mom? In this world I can see! So many colors, shades, and shapes. It's amazing! I can fly in this place! Don't know how I got here though. I just remember pain, and something picking me up with rough cold hands. But that doesn't matter I can see! I am so happy to *see* you!" John's voice trailed off into silence. Celest turned to see what it was that John was staring at. It was just your average sunrise. When she turned back around, she saw that the feathers beneath John's eyes were dark with moisture, and his golden eyes were over bright.

She gave him a sad smile. "Your first sunrise," she said quietly as a tear rolled down her own face.

A little while later, the two siblings fell asleep curled into warm balls on Stormy's back. Celest found herself in the corner of her bedroom watching her four-year-old self, who was just getting finished with her bed time story. She was a very cute kid with her long, thick, black hair pulled up in pig tails. Her almond eyes sparkled with the love she felt from, and for her mother. After her mom uttered the words, "…and they lived happily ever after. The end," the younger Celest asked, "Please tell me about Dad again. I never really get to see him…Please!"

After a second or two her mom smiled and spoke softly, "Your dad is a kind man, and he loves you very much. He has told me how much he wishes he could see you more."

The expression on her small face was difficult to read as she asked, "How did you guys meet?"

Mrs. Windheart went silent as she relived a gentle and sweet memory, then she spoke in a distant voice, "It was raining that day we met."

Celest awoke with a heavy heart; it had been three years since she had that dream—why now? She noticed that they were no longer snoozing on Stormy's back, but were now in a sunlit room with two round fluffy beds. On the other bed in a nest of blankets was John, who was just waking up himself. Upon leaving their room they saw a tiny man who had jewel colored wings. He stood no more than three inches high. As soon as he saw the two siblings he waved for them to sit down to breakfast. Celest was just thinking how strange it was that fairies might exist when the little man spoke, "I have been requested to be your guide. Just call me Oscar as my real name is far too hard to pronounce."

Celest wondered if it would be rude to ask, but could not resist. So, as politely as she could, she asked, "Are you a fairy?"

Oscar began to laugh, "Well now, that all depends. Do you believe that if you were to squeeze me hard enough you could get three wishes? And would that eagle try to eat me just for being smaller than three inches?"

Celest giggled, and trying not to laugh too hard she answered, "No, and this is my brother, John. So he wouldn't be interested in eating you at all."

Oscar gave her a wink and grinned, "Then I suppose I am! And I know all about your brother." He made a gesture toward an intricate gold crown sitting a top his curly black locks, "Actually, there are some fairies who would call me king." Oscar then gave the two a deep bow and said, "Please enjoy your breakfast. When you are finished we will discuss other things." The table at which John and Celest now sat was eight feet by eight feet. It was covered with every fruit known to man, and dozens that were not.

In tall glasses for the children to drink was ice cold water both sweet and pure.

Half an hour later, a completely stuffed Celest watched her brother as he pecked at a blue, water-bottle shaped melon. When he was done he looked up at Celest and said, "That was awesome. It tasted just like a supreme pizza!"

Oscar looked puzzled as he asked, "What is a supreme pizza?"

It was Celest who answered him, "It's a human food from Italy. You said that 'we will discuss other things'. What did you have in mind, Oscar?"

He smiled at her, "Ah, straight to the heart of the matter. Just like a workaholic thunder horse I know." Oscar nodded in Stormy's direction, and took his seat on a banana. "I have heard from a most reliable source that there is a creature that has something to do with you. It has recently taken up residence in the JaPoyPoy forest. As soon as you are ready we will be on our way there."

FLIGHT TO JaPoyPoy Forest

John was wondering what would be waiting for them when they got there. Would there be more fantastic things that had nothing to do with the world he had come from, a world he had only dreamed of seeing? Would it be safe and tranquil, or perhaps there were threats in this world that remained hidden…waiting.

His musings were brought to a stop when from Stormy's head Oscar called back to him and Celest, "We will be there soon. One thing I must warn you not to do, is do not pull the green PoyPoy plant's dangling vine. As tempting as it may be, it is an illusion designed by the plant to get you to do just that. If you do, then you are going to be slimed and then eaten. Don't worry, you will be fine. Just make sure you keep me and 'Stormy', did you call him, in sight at all times."

As they landed with a soft thud and dismounted from Stormy's back, the forest seemed to come to life. Buzzing, chirping, and…roaring filled the air. John, feeling a little anxious, flew back to sit on Celest's shoulder which earlier that day, Oscar had attached a padding that he said was thick Zooza hide. He told her that John's talons were razor sharp, and that this would protect her if she ever wanted to give him a ride. Stormy lead the way and Oscar took up the rear. In spite of the fact that this world was so alien to her, Celest felt very secure and at ease.

The deeper they got into the forest, the less sunlight was able to penetrate the forest's canopy. About two miles into the forest, they were engulfed in a sort of twilight. Green vines were dangling all around them; each had a strange blue glow. Celest could feel John's grip tighten as she approached one. There was a flash of red light, and then a picture of Mrs. Windheart appeared within a golden frame. Celest was just about to reach for it when John yelled, "Don't touch it!" It was not a photo that he saw, but a fat red ball covered with spiky tentacles. As if their minds were connected somehow, Celest's trance was broken, and she saw the thing for what it was.

"What was that *monster*?" she asked Oscar as they pressed on.

Oscar gave her a grim nod, "Monster is right. That was the PoyPoy plant I told you about. They give me the creeps and I've been here several times."

Celest fell into quiet thought for a few moments and then broke the silence, "How was John able to see through the illusion?"

Oscar took his time thinking about it before his answer came, "I only have two likely answers, one or both of which could be correct. The first possibility is that his eyes are special; he is no ordinary golden eagle. This is saying a lot as the golden eagles of this realm are incredibly powerful creatures by their own right. Second, the plants use visual illusions of things they somehow know will tempt their pray. As John has never seen anything until recently, he just wants to see period. This may have made the plant feel that just letting him see it at all was bait enough."

Deeper and deeper they pressed into the forest. More than once Celest could have sworn she saw something darting in and out of the shadows, but only out of the corner of her eyes. Whenever she tried to look at whatever it was directly, there was nothing there except a piece of the forest's tranquil scenery void of life, except for a few bugs here and there. After another half hour of walking, loud roars could be heard as if they were but twenty feet away. Celest wondered what angry creature could be making such a racket.

Just as they pushed through a thick wall of vines they saw a silver orangutan running from a large group of wolves that were the size of small pickup trucks. He had a small log hanging from his mouth, and he looked like...he was having the time of his life. Celest's thoughts were drawn to her youngest brother, Eric, for some reason. Just as she realized that the last time her thoughts were so strongly drawn to her family, Celest had found John, Stormy had rushed between the monkey and the wolves. He reared up onto his hind legs and spread his wings as lighting began to arc in and out of his body. Thunder filled the air and the wolves ran off with their tails between their legs. As he was running past her, the leader went to take a piece of Celest with him. She was so frightened that she closed her eyes. Without knowing why, she raised her right hand in the direction of the head wolf. A powerful gust of wind sent the wolves flying through the forest, bouncing off trees and rocks as they went. Oscar gave Celest a knowing look and smiled, "We should be off. We have your youngest brother and that is all we came here for."

Oscar pointed up at the tree canopy and the trees leaned out of the way revealing the starlit sky. Celest laughed as Eric swung back and forth hanging off of Stormy's tail before flipping up and landing on his back. Eric fell asleep right away. Celest on the other hand, was far too happy to sleep. The warmth she felt in her stomach from finally being reunited with both her brothers out stripped the fact that she did not know exactly how she got the wind to listen to her. Celest crawled up behind Oscar and tapped him on his little shoulder, "What are we going to do next? Do you know how to get me and my brothers back home to our mom?"

Oscar looked like he was getting ready to drop a piece of bad news. It looked as though his words were going to fail him, but he finally found his voice, "There is a problem with that, you see. While I definitely know the way, there is an obstacle like none you could imagine. This world is in balance with the one you come from. There is a monster of sorts here that feeds on chaos. Naturally, it gains strength from imbalance. It was he that opened the portal that brought you here. It was he that kidnapped Eric from pre-school, and John from the hospital. While your presence here does not create imbalance, it is the fact that you cannot stop his minions from reeking havoc in your world that does."

The first words out of Celest's mouth after hearing this were, "Is my mom safe?"

Oscar answered at once, "Yes, the cowards will not act

until you and your brothers are no threat at all. The next place we must go to is my kingdom. I have arranged for a house to be built to accommodate your size. Don't worry, we will not be staying there too long. We just need to get you ready for the journey ahead. We will get you home, and no harm will come to your mother—I promise."

Celest awoke in a cold sweat. She had the dream again, but this time it was different. A huge, scaly claw cloaked in shadow broke into her room right at the end of her dream and was trying to grab her mother. Breaking free from the nightmare, she looked around to see a huge city made up of a great, but very miniature, castle surrounded by tiny buildings that seemed to be created out of colorful dollhouses. Eight feet from the border of the city was a quaint little cottage, with beautiful stained glass windows, each depicting a flower of some type. Beside the cottage, a little water fall misted the air with rainbows.

John noticed how Celest awoke with an uneasy look on her face. "Are you all right, Celest?" She looked around, and seeing that everyone was safe, she smiled at John and nodded. Knowing his sister was okay, excitement filled his voice. "Take a look at this place! It's beautiful, huh? We're in Oscar's kingdom. It is called Bulaklak Haven."

She shook her head trying to clear it before she called up to Oscar, "What exactly are we going to do to get ready? Is it going to take very long? I've got this bad feeling that time is running out. I am afraid that this monster might not wait to get us before going after our world... our mom."

Oscar was concerned at how tired Celest looked. He

gently flew from atop Stormy's head back to Celest and handed her a dark blue leaf. "We will be here maybe a few days. It would take anyone else, including powerful fairies, several months to master their powers and push them to the needed levels. You, on the other hand, have natural talent, and I have no doubt that you will be an excellent student. Suck on that leaf until dinner is ready. It will give you energy and you'll need it. You've got a long day ahead of you."

Celest asked blankly, "My powers? I don't have powers...unless...you mean when I got the wind to listen me?" Oscar said nothing but smiled all the same.

The children slid off the massive and powerful back of the great storm stallion, before following Oscar into the quaint cottage they had been admiring. It had a beautiful oak table and three rooms beside the kitchen. Each had the same type of big, fluffy, and round bed that Celest and John had used before. At this point however, it was the three bathrooms that they were interested in. They were clean, bejeweled, and the fact that it had been a lengthy trip also added to their appeal.

Gifts Of Bulaklak Haven

They had arrived at Oscar's kingdom around eight in the morning. Celest assumed that since they had not heard from anyone since then, they were being given the day to get settled in. At four o'clock that afternoon, the sound of wind chimes indicated that there was someone at the door. Celest opened the door as John landed on her shoulder. On the other side hovered a fairy woman with long, dark hair and sapphire colored eyes.

She gave the two a deep bow and spoke. "You are requested to come and have dinner with the king in the castle courtyard at seven. I have," she waved her hand in the air and three boxes flew to hover in front of Celest, "dinner gifts from the king. He requests that you have them on when you arrive." Celest held out her arms and the boxes placed themselves gently in them. She told the fairy that it would be their pleasure, and went inside.

The top box had her name on it. Celest popped loose the ribbon which was held in place by a wax seal of the royal crest (two crossed roses with a broad sword pointing down between them). Inside was a beautiful golden ring with an emerald as its center piece, and tiny diamonds surrounded the emerald forming words in what she could only guess was the fairies' native language. Celest put it on her right ring finger. It was a perfect fit. Next she opened John's gift for him. It was a dazzling platinum necklace that fit him like a harness. The centerpiece of this one was blue topaz, and it too, was surrounded by the same diamond lettering that his sister's ring had.

John looking down at his chest asked his older sister, "Do you think there is more to these things than just looking good?"

Celest shrugged and said, "Who knows? Let's open Eric's in his room." The two got up and went to Eric's room. They found him sleeping with his feet holding a pillow in the air above his head. When they opened the last box they found a silver headband inside. In its center was a golden pearl. Again, the same diamond-formed words surrounded the center piece. Celest gently put the band on Eric's head and left his room. Once Celest taught him how, she and John played a game of rummy with a deck of cards she had found in the kitchen. John had to keep his cards on the table behind a stack of books, as he had no hands to speak of. After a few games, it was seven o'clock before they knew it.

Once again, the young fairy woman came to their door. This time it was to escort them to dinner. She gave the three siblings an appraising look and smiled, "Those charms suit you very well. If you are ready, dinner awaits." She bowed and took to the air right in front of Celest.

John was perched on Celest's shoulder and she took

Eric by the hand. They followed the fairy to the castle's courtyard where there was a big table with a doll-sized table at its head. Both of the tables had been covered with food, everything from steaks and pheasants to ice-cream cakes and pies were ready to be eaten. Oscar was sitting at the miniscule table at the head. He smiled and once again waved for them to sit and eat.

Celest returned the smile and said, "Thank you." Then Celest and her brothers sat down to a magnificent banquet. Two hours later it seemed to Celest that her waist band had shrunk at least two sizes. Celest covered her mouth as she burped, and then said, "Oscar, when will we start our training? As good as this dinner was, it would have tasted a lot better had I known that my brothers and I would be home with our mom soon. Also I have a question, one that I feel I should have asked you way earlier. Why did my brothers change when they entered this world? And why did I not?"

Oscar nodded and said, "You'll start your training at dawn. And as to your mystery about the form changing, John and Eric simply became what they were supposed to be. John became a golden eagle because he simply deserves to see. Eric became a monkey, because he has strength and curiosity that made this form fit him the best. The reason you kept your human form will be revealed to you in due time. And by the by, you guys look great in those gifts I sent you. I made them myself three years ago. Each can only be removed if their owner wills it. They all provide protection against poisons and harmful infections. As a bonus they keep people, with the ability, from controlling your minds. Meaning you cannot be brainwashed, confused by magic, or controlled by supernatural means what so ever. Now, Celest, I have something else I need to give you." Oscar held up his right hand and a group of five fairies flew up to the table carrying a reversible cloak.

It was magenta on one side, and royal blue on the other. As soon as it was placed into Celest's hands, Oscar spoke, "This cloak will keep you cool in intense heat, and warm in the coldest of weather. It is indestructible and will protect against any type of elemental attack." Celest was at a loss for words, she had received two beautiful gifts in one evening. She looked up at Oscar but still could not speak. He smiled at her and said, "You're very welcome. I suggest that you get off to bed. You have an early start tomorrow."

Celest's dream led her down the now familiar path that she had come to walk each time she went to sleep. She was just about to ask her mom to tell her about her dad, when a monstrous wing, dripping with shadow swooped in through the wall and grabbed Mrs. Windheart around the waist. Wind chimes could be heard in the distance. With each chime, the shadow engulfed wing lowered her mom to the ground. Just as it vanished, Celest woke up and discovered that there was someone at the door. It was Oscar himself.

"Did you rest well?" he asked as he stepped over the threshold. Celest's heart was still pounding but she answered yes anyway. After she and her brothers had some toast, he led them off to a forest clearing. There were large stone, bucket-shaped, vessels all over the place. In some there was fine sand, and in others there was water. All around the clearing there were torches burning brightly.

"Celest, you and your brothers have special powers. It is my happy job to teach you how to use them. Good Morning, sir!" Oscar bowed with a chuckle as Stormy trotted over to watch the Windheart children begin training. "Celest, we will start with you. Would you please stand in front of me? That's right. Now, your abilities seem to give you dominion over the elements: water, fire, earth, wind and so forth. To see exactly where you are in terms of control, I want you to have a freestyle session. Just focus on what you want to see done. You have the four main elements around you right now...go for it." Oscar stepped out of the way.

Celest took in her environment and imagined it bending to her will. The sand was carried out of one of the buckets by a gust of spinning air and hovered twelve feet in front of her. Then streams of fire spiraled in from three of the torches turning the sand into molten glass. It slowly became shaped like a big magnifying glass as a cool mist floated out of the water buckets. The mist floated over to the hot glass and slowly cooled it so that it could keep its shape. The lens gently lowered itself to the ground, as the sound of clapping filled the air. Celest turned to see Stormy nodding his approval and Oscar smiling.

When Oscar spoke his voice shook with pride, "I knew you had natural talent, but never, not even in my wildest dreams did I expect you to have such control. I think that if you just practice on your own a bit you'll be fine. Just make sure that you do practice. Well, that saves us some time." Oscar nodded and his gaze shifted from Celest to a near by tree. "John if you will please step...or should I say please fly forward. Thanks."

MATTERS OF THE HEART

John perched himself on one of the rims of the now empty buckets. Oscar turned and called off into the woods, "Marlene, it is time for you to test John!" Seconds later the same fairy who had led them to dinner the night before flew into the clearing.

She gave John a curtsy, and then looked deep into his eyes while she spoke, "Your eyes are special. They can see through any illusion, see into hearts, and can see that which cannot be seen at all. Now…if you can, find my true self!" In less time than it takes to blink an eye, fifty more Marlenes seemed to appear out of thin air. Each began to fly at high speed around John's head leaving a trail of red light in their wake. John's eyes narrowed with concentration as he took to the air. He glided back and forth, the fairy cloud around him growing brighter and brighter. John did a back flip in midair before diving straight to the ground. His talons closed on air, but two by two the cloud that was Marlene faded away. Laughter filled the air as the real Marlene appeared beneath John's foot, his sharp talons surrounding, but not touching her. She was pinned stomach down, and was laughing so hard her face was flushed.

"I think like his sister, John has also a firm grasp on his powers," she called to Oscar while wiping a tear from her left cheek.

Oscar cleared his throat and said, "Eric's special abilities include super strength and agility. He will not be tested. Doing so could get him hurt. He's not even two years old, after all. Now back to the courtyard for some lunch!" John let Marlene up as the others marched ahead.

Once the others were out of ear shot John spoke quietly, "Marlene, wait. I did not mean to look as deeply as I did but...why don't you tell Oscar how you feel?" Marlene froze on the spot.

It seemed like she was not going to say anything at all. At last, however, she sighed and responded, "He could never love me...he is a king. I'm just a castle servant."

John thought quietly for a moment, and suddenly laughed as an idea popped into his head. "I could look at him for you! Then I could tell you how he feels about you!"

The tiny woman shook her head and patted him on the wing, "No, knowing one way or the other would break my heart. To find out he does love me would only hurt because we can never be together. And if I were to find out he feels nothing for me..." Marlene fell into silence as they followed the others to their afternoon meal. It was on that day that John learned how complicated matters of the heart could be. Be it fairy or human, the heart is a mystery all on its own.

They all enjoyed a meal of roasted chicken and bar-bequed hamburgers. As Celest finished her second burger, Oscar smiled brightly and said, "You see I know *some* things about your world!"

Celest smiled in return and said, "You sure do!" John nodded in agreement as Eric popped two into his mouth at once. This time it was not ice water that they had to drink but a dark blue juice. Celest took a sip out of her cup and gave Oscar a quizzical look as she asked, "You guys actually have a juice here that tastes like root beer?"

Oscar laughed, "Oh no, that drink is called zana. It comes from the melon your brother said tasted like 'supreme pizza.' It is called the kaholoholo melon. It grows on a group of islands called Janjoe, which reside in our version of your Pacific Ocean. Zana, like the melon it comes from, is very good for you. But, this particular fruit does not have its own flavor and takes on the taste of whatever its consumer might be craving. In your case it tastes like root beer."

Celest took another sip then said, "So, this drink tastes different to everyone. John, what does yours taste like?"

John dipped his beak into his drinking bowl and looked at his sister, "Chocolate milkshakes!" Celest laughed as she got up to ask Stormy if he wanted to go for a walk. Stormy nodded yes and Celest thanked Oscar for the magnificent lunch before they set off.

Celest followed Stormy about three miles away from Bulaklak Haven to a tranquil lake. It was so vast that the other side was barely visible. There was a rickety sign on the shore that they had arrived on that said, "To you, who visit, enjoy the peace. If you hunger, for bait, use cheese. But if you are wise, ignore you will, that alluring sound…the siren's trill." After reading these words Celest shrugged her shoulders and said, "Who knew that the stuff my world would call fairy tales, in your world, are just common fact?" She smiled at Stormy for a moment before kicking off her shoes to sit with her feet touching the lakes edge. She felt that this was as good a time as any to practice with her powers. She looked at the surface of the lake eight feet in front of her, and imagined statues of water forming, which she would shape into the likeness of her family. In mere moments, great flowing statues rose out of the lake's surface. Eric and John were in their human forms standing next to a statue of Celest. Their mother's statue was standing right behind her three children. When Celest turned to tell Stormy about her family, she was shocked to see that great tears shimmered gently in his eyes. As Celest returned the watery statues to their natural state it began to rain. Stormy extended one of his great wings over Celest, it kept her dry more effectively than any umbrella could have done. She patted him on his side and said, "Let's go. The others might be wondering what's taking us so long to get back."

Together they returned to Bulaklak Haven. Upon returning, Celest told Oscar what had happened at the lake, and the glimmer of sadness she thought she saw in Stormy's eyes. To her surprise, the news did not surprise Oscar in the slightest. He looked at her and said, "You must have reminded him of his own family with those statues of yours. Do you remember that monster that I told you about? As long as it is free to do as it pleases, Stormy's children are in danger. They are such powerful creatures that it has marked them as a threat." Celest remembered how powerful and frightening Stormy had looked when he stood between Eric and the wolves. In her opinion, if his children had inherited *any* of his power, it was no wonder this thing was nervous—especially if it is as sinister as it sounds. Because from what she saw, Stormy, although good and gentle, is a force to be reckoned with if his friends are endangered.

THE VILLAGE OF ICE

The next day Oscar announced that it was time to get going. Their first stop would be the dwelling place of the creature that dragged Celest and her brothers into this world. Oscar smiled as John ruffled his feathers with uneasiness. "Not to worry, we could not get inside right now even if Stormy and I thought you were ready. You'll see what I mean soon enough." Celest, Eric, and John mounted Stormy's back as Oscar said goodbye to Marlene. The castle guards announced their departure with a long mournful note on a series of different brass instruments. Before they had time to stop enjoying the pleasant scenery of Bulaklak Haven, it was suddenly drifting out of sight into the horizon. They flew on and on, day turned into night, and then into dawn again.

Celest had her usual dark dream. This time, however, the beast did not enter her room. But she could still see its eyes floating beyond her window. Its body was so shrouded in darkness that she could not see what it truly looked like. When Celest awoke she was informed by John that they would be there soon. *So,* Celest began to think, *is this world that we're on...still earth? And what is the name of this monster causing all this trouble?*

She voiced her questions to Oscar, who looked very impressed that she had thought to ask. He smiled and said, "This is a world that exists in a dimension parallel to yours. Our world and earth are one and the same, but divided onto two planes. Our portion has no name, because many feel that would put unnecessary limitations on our world's existence. As to the name of our foe, it simply calls itself the Oblivion King."

Even though it was now ten o'clock in the morning, the sun seemed to disappear from the sky. Oscar pointed to a shape in the distance that was darker than the enchanted night that now engulfed them. His face hardened as he spoke, "This is home to that foul creature you are destined to destroy. As you can now see, it is surrounded by a sphere, or force field if you will, of concentrated darkness. Darkness in itself is not evil and allows anyone, good or bad, to pass through it freely. But this darkness is different. It is wielded by the dark king himself, and will not allow anyone but his most trusted through its gates. I have word that he has creatures serving him, and that their job is to create as much chaos and pain as possible. The negative energy they create is siphoned directly to their master. Now, the dark king only keeps a small portion for himself, the rest he devotes to his barrier. So, as soon as we have stopped his servants' activities, the barrier should be weakened enough for us to get through, and hopefully he will be weakened himself."

Celest nodded and said, "At least we have a plan. Do you know where any of these 'servants' are now?"

Oscar gave her a grim smile as he answered, "The first one we are going after is currently tormenting the village of Rose Brew. The others will be easily found. Just look where there is the most suffering and hardship going on and that's where they will be."

John spoke in a determined voice, "To Rose Brew!" Stormy whinnied loudly, but it is not known if he was agreeing with John or if it was because Eric had just slapped him on the rear really *hard*. Either way, Stormy headed in Rose Brew's direction with a burst of speed.

John had mixed feelings about going home, although he knew that was exactly what he wanted to do. He sat in silence at the very rear of Stormy's back, staring into the twilit horizon behind them. Eric crawled behind Celest and promptly fell asleep. Oscar could be heard talking with Stormy. "Well, it looks like we're off on another one of our adventures again. I never thought that we would have such young children as our allies, though. Don't worry, old friend, I'm sure we can keep them safe."

Celest, John, and Eric were all asleep when they arrived at Rose Brew. They were awakened not by Oscar, but by the intense cold that filled the air. Eric's fur seemed enough to keep him warm, and John fluffed his feathers and they kept him warm enough. Celest, on the other hand, had to don the cloak Oscar had given her. She wore it with the blue side out, and pulled its hood on. Warmth filled her body. She turned to thank Oscar for the gift again, but the words got lost on the way to her mouth, she instead asked, "Why is it so cold here?"

Oscar answered as he charmed his clothing to keep

the cold out, "The servant of the dark one—he is an ice dragon, a great flying serpent. We had better inform the village elder of our presence. She would like to know why we have come." Stormy landed as soft as a feather would upon a lake's surface. John fluttered to one of Celest's padded shoulders as she hopped off Stormy's back. She reached up to helped Eric down. Together they followed Oscar to a green chateau that seemed to be at the very center of the village. Everyone except Stormy stepped onto the front porch, and it was Celest who knocked. An elfin woman answered and asked them in. She barely cleared five feet tall with mocha skin, and her ears came to gentle points. Her eyes were as emerald as Celest's ring, and her smile was so warm that it seemed quite out of place in such a brutally cold environment. She looked like she was maybe twenty-five years old but, as her kind does not grow old, she could have very well been eight hundred years old instead. She asked them all to sit down on a couch that was draped in a blue satin blanket. She then stepped out of the room and returned with steaming cups of hot chocolate. Each cup was very creamy, topped off with marshmallows, and had a cinnamon stick which not only could be used for stirring the cocoa, but added a certain something that made the drink taste that much better.

"It is so nice to have guests again. But, I am afraid you have come at a time when our village not only looks the worst it has in many, many years, but is also the most dangerous it has *ever* been. I must ask you to leave as soon as you can. You may stay at my home as long as you must before you go, but please go soon. My name is Terra and I am the—"

The young looking elder's sentence was finished by Oscar, "The village elder." Oscar then turned his attention to the obviously concerned elfin woman, "We know that your village is suffering, and by whose hands. My friends and I are on a mission; one that requires the liberation of your home town in order to succeed. We are quite aware of the dangers, but we *do* have both the power and desire to help."

Terra took a moment to consider Oscar's words. After a moment she spoke, "I am thankful that you want to help but, I cannot endanger children. Not even children who are presently transformed into powerful animals." Celest was amazed; no one had told Terra that the eagle and orangutan with them used to be her human brothers. She had thought that Terra gave them something to drink simply because she liked animals.

Oscar smiled at the elf, "You are very perceptive. The children before you have a destiny, and it is to smite the Oblivion King himself, and all who serve his evil ways. Elves are one of the creatures able to speak the various tongues of the animals. Question John and Eric yourself, though, Eric is not much of a conversationalist yet."

Celest was just about to ask why it would matter that Terra could speak the animal's different tongues when Terra spoke to John, "Do you think it wise to challenge such a powerful foe? Do you think you have the power to *topple* such a foe?"

John looked her square in the eyes, "The dark king is a monster that needs taking down. If we don't have the power to stop him, then we will find it!" Terra seemed satisfied with his answer.

Celest turned to Oscar and asked him the question she

had meant to earlier. He smiled as he always did when Celest asked him a question. "You can communicate with Eric and John because you are brothers and sister. Because you are family you can naturally understand the golden eagle and orangutan languages, just as if your brothers were speaking English. If any one outside your family, like me for example, wanted to understand what your brothers were saying they would have to speak the languages of the animals your brothers currently are."

Terra waited for Oscar to finish talking before she turned to Celest and asked her, "Do you agree with your brother? I do sense power within you, but will you be able to bring it to the surface in time?"

Celest looked Terra in her eyes, just as John had done earlier, and spoke with a quiet passion. "John is right. We will stop this chaotic monster. It must be done to protect our mother, and the world for that matter. Our powers seem to be coming along just fine, and we will push them as far as we need to."

Again the elder seemed to be happy with the answer she was given. She walked to the window and spoke as she watched the snow begin to fall outside. "I have not seen anyone with your kind of courage at least for a millennia or so, and never were they as young as you. I have no doubt that you will do what the fairy king says you are destined to. The ice dragon comes every month or so, and it has been about a month since his last 'visit.' He may be here in a few weeks, so I suggest that you rest up, train, and plan while you wait for him. He's a fearsome foe."

The Ice Dragon

The next day the Windheart children awoke at eight o'clock in the morning. Celest was happy to get a break from the dream that had recently taken to haunting her. Instead of monstrous creatures, that night she had dreamed of floating around the world sitting inside a giant puffball, while eating cookies and drinking ice cold milk. Being relieved that this morning was not tainted by dark memories from the night before, she just laid there relaxing, while letting the sun warm her light brown skin. Feeling that this was an excellent way for her day to start, she told her brothers that it was time to go downstairs. Eric must have been the first to smell the food, because he rushed ahead of Celest and John laughing all the way to the table. Celest and John suddenly realized why Eric was so hyped to get to breakfast. The smell of fat sausages sizzling on an iron skillet filled their nostrils. When they reached the dining room they found Eric happily eating his breakfast. Oscar was leaning against a milk jug merrily chatting with Terra, who smiled as the other two siblings took their seats. The sausages they had smelled was only the beginning. Terra had made waffles, pancakes, cheese omelets, and bacon as well. Terra had given them fresh cold orange juice to drink with their breakfast.

"Good morning. Did you get enough sleep?" Terra asked as she poured some juice into a bowl for John to drink from.

John tasted the juice before he answered, "We slept great, and thanks for making us breakfast."

When they were finished eating breakfast they decided to go for a walk, and see what Stormy was up to. Celest felt nice and warm in her cloak, which today she wore with the magenta side out. As they walked along, Eric picked up handfuls of snow just to watch them melt slowly in his hands. John flew ahead, while Oscar fondly watched them all from behind.

"Morning Stormy!" John said as he landed on a frozen tree stump. Stormy greeted John by nuzzling him. The stump was so slippery with ice that John would have slipped off the other side had it not been for his sharp talons.

John laughed as he said, "You're going to knock me off. Everyone will be here soon, you think we should practice?" It only took three minutes for everyone to arrive after Stormy had nodded yes. Celest waved hello as Eric rushed forward to hug Stormy's right front leg.

Oscar allowed the happy mood to continue for a moment before he spoke, "We do not know how much time we have until the ice dragon arrives. We had better spend what time we do have training." Oscar smiled slightly as he reached down and made a little snowball.

After tossing it into the air and catching it a few times he said, "But…that does not mean that we can't have a good time doing it!" Oscar laughed as he threw it at John. The once small snowball grew to the size of a soft ball as it tumbled through the air.

John barely had time to dodge it as he flew out of the way. He paused in midair for a moment before he yelled, "Snow ball fight!" and dived behind a snow mound. Celest held her right hand out to the side, and a crunching noise filled the air as all the snow on the ground around her turned into snowballs. John soared out from behind the mound holding a snowball in each of his feet. Oscar threw two more of his growing snowballs at Celest. Although her eyes were currently focused on John, who was rushing her, she saw them out of the corner of her eyes. Eleven snowballs floated into the air around her, two of them took out the snowballs that Oscar had just thrown at her. A third one hurled itself at Oscar himself, but he vanished in a flash of light before it could make contact. He then appeared on Stormy's back and decided to watch from the side lines. Celest turned her full attention to John, and eight snowballs shot at him. Through a display of impressive aerobatics, he managed to dodge seven of the snowballs in the barrage Celest sent his way. He had just gotten close enough to deliver his cold pay load when the eighth snow ball hit him on the chest causing him to drop one of his snowballs. John released his other snowball just in time to hit Celest on her right shoulder. It seemed to be a tie, but no one was watching Eric. He was busy making his "snow ball" while everyone else was caught up in the game. Celest turned in time to see him toss his snow ball at John. The only problem was that it was more of a snow boulder than a snowball. John was slapped out of the air and then buried in a pile of snow. Celest cleared away the snow with a gust of wind to reveal a stunned John. Everyone was so surprised that they just stood there blinking. The confused silence lasted for a couple of minutes before everyone collapsed with laughter.

As soon as everyone had caught their breath, they all headed back to Terra's house. After spending the day out in the frigid wasteland, stepping into her house was like stepping into paradise. The cold weather outside seemed unable to cross her threshold, even when her door was opened wide for them to enter. On their way in, Terra stopped Oscar and Celest to give them velvet pajamas along with long cotton robes that went down to their feet. She gave the entire group a smile, "Hope you're hungry from practice! Dinner will be ready in an hour or so. If you will kindly go upstairs and get washed up…" As they disappeared around the corner leading to the stairs Terra called after them, "Celest! King Oscar! Just leave your dirty clothes in the hamper. I'll have them cleaned and ready by morning."

Oscar flew back down the stairs and said, "There is no need for you to do our laundry for us. We can take care of it ourselves." Terra seemed to be so happy to have company that she refused to take no for an answer. Oscar said thank you in a defeated voice before heading up stairs to get cleaned up. In the time it took to get everyone ready for dinner, dinner had been finished cooking. Terra continued to prove herself as an excellent hostess; dinner that night was extraordinary. They had broiled ribs which had been rubbed down with lemon pepper, a tender pot roast with carrot slices, green beans, and potatoes in the gravy.

Terra also seemed to know that broccoli, while by itself is only tolerable, is actually really good when drenched in melted cheese. The Windheart children were also pleased to see that to drink was ice cold zana.

When they had finished eating dinner Oscar turned to Terra and said, "Thank you very much. That was an amazing meal! You know, the way you've been making sure that Celest, Eric and John have been well fed, it makes me think that you will make a wonderful mother one day." Terra's face fell at these words, and Oscar's was overcome with concern. He spoke softly, "Sorry...I had no idea...you are a mother? If anything I said caused you pain I'm very sorry. I did not mean to open old wounds."

Terra's voice did not even crack in the slightest when she spoke, but the pain, etched deep in her emerald eyes, showed that it was costing her dearly not to break down in tears, "It's okay. There was no way you could have known. As you know, King Oscar, my people are as timeless as your own. Having children is not something we can just do, because our offspring cannot die of old age we are only permitted to have three. Fourteen years ago, I decided to have my first child. My husband is...was a very good man. The year before last, the ice dragon came; he carried both my husband and my son off to their deaths. I very much doubt that I will ever see my husband, Charles, or my son, Alexander, ever again. This is one of the reasons I am so anxious for you to crush the Oblivion King. I'm Sorry, no pressure."

Oscar told the children that it was time for bed. Once they were upstairs he turned to Terra and said, "Your husband and child will be avenged. If you can, take comfort in that fact. I hope that you can at least have pleasant dreams to distract you from your pain tonight."

Celest stayed awake for two hours after she laid down, thinking about Terra and how much pain she had to live with every day. Slowly she drifted off to sleep. Celest's mom had just finished reading her a bedtime story when the walls around her began to whisper madly, "Soon, soon, soon, soon your time in existence will be cut short…meddling fools…children are no match for the likes of *me*!"

Celest awoke in a cold sweat; she noticed that at the foot of her bed her things were all neatly folded. She picked up her stuff and got ready for another day of training. It was immediately apparent that last night's conversation with Oscar did not make Terra any less hospitable. When Celest and her brothers got to the kitchen they found a large plate full of sliced fruits and a bowl of strawberry yogurt at its center for dipping. Also, Terra had put out a large plate of bagels and a saucer of cream cheese, along with glasses and a jug of milk. Terra was in the living room talking with Oscar who had apparently finished eating. When John, Eric, and Celest were finished eating they sat on the couch and looked expectantly to Oscar.

He smiled at them and said, "Today we will be preparing for the dragon's arrival. Terra has just told me that there are two houses here no one lives in anymore. We will make piles of wood all around the area. They will be doused in lamp oil and all the piles will be connected by ropes soaked in the same lamp oil. The wood, as I am sure you have already guessed, is coming from the abandoned houses."

When Celest heard about the abandoned houses, a thought occurred to her, "Terra, why have I not seen anyone else but you in this village?"

Terra smiled at her in the same way Oscar did whenever she had a question. She walked over to sit by Celest as she spoke, "The members of this village, who have managed to survive the ice dragon's wrath so far, prefer the safety of their homes rather than the dangerous world beyond their doors. They rarely leave that sense of security that they feel inside their homes, even if it is a false one. Not to mention the fact that living in constant fear makes them wary of strangers, even ones as nice as you."

Time passes quickly when you're busy. The next five days seemed to pass in a blur. The Windheart children used their powers the best ways they knew how in order to make the plan succeed. John flew high and helped decide on the best places to put the bonfires. And when the abandoned houses were no more, he helped find dead trees to make the bonfires larger. Celest used her elemental powers to clear large areas of moisture and ice so that the fires burned as brightly and as hot as they possibly could. Eric was, in fact, the main reason the deserted houses were already torn down. They just let him play as roughly as he wanted to, and when a child has super strength at his disposal, he can play pretty rough.

At the end of the sixth day, Terra threw a huge party. However this party was not being held in her house but in the village square. They set up a huge gazebo which covered the entire square. Oscar had spent the day putting charms on it to keep the freezing wind from entering it. The Windhearts were asked to place invitations on all the doors and knock before moving on to the next house. Terra, of course, did her thing in the kitchen creating a vast array of dishes. Many of which were new to the Windhearts.

When it was time for the party, there was an eighteen by thirty foot table set at the center of the gazebo. There was everything on it from speared meat roasted on an open fire, to a violently-purple pudding that tasted like hot apple pie and vanilla ice cream with bits of hot fudge brownies floating around in it. This night was to be the extravagant precursor to the party that the people of Rose Brew would hold when they were at last freed from the ice dragon's grasp. That night was the first time anyone belonging to Celest's party had been able to see the other inhabitants of the village. Rose Brew held a beautiful array of elves. There were at least one hundred and fifty elves that showed up for the pre-celebration. The elves were as diverse as the human race when it came to different physical features: dark and light complexions, short and tall, scrawny and well-muscled elves filled the gazebo. Everyone was having a great time. The music and food lasted well into the night. When the party was over, the elves all toasted Terra for her kindness, and the Windhearts for their courage. The party lasted so long that when the Windheart children did get to sleep, they did not wake up until three in the afternoon the next day. When they did get up, Terra told them that she had received word that the dragon would be arriving that night.

At four o'clock Oscar went out to light the bonfires. "When we face him it will be on our terms, not his." he muttered to himself on the way out the front door. Celest went to her room to switch her pajamas for her protective cloak and padded shirt. Hours passed, but the dragon did not show up. John was worried that they may have started the fires too soon, but to his surprise Oscar told him that they did such a good job with the fires, that they had only grown stronger in the past few hours.

It happened just as Terra's clock struck eleven o'clock. A great howling wind began to rage outside. Celest said, "It's time." as she walked out the front door.

Oscar nodded and went out next. Eric and John followed suit. Once they were outside, a great twisting shadow could be seen in the distance. It was growing larger as it grew nearer. John barely had time to wonder if they were ready when their foe was suddenly just two miles in front of them. Its scales looked like they were made of ice crystals. Its fangs were like cruel scimitars hewn from ice. Its body was long and flowing, and its large pale green eyes were even more frightening as they reflected the bonfire's light and the light from the full moon in the sky.

It was Eric who acted first as he picked up a chunk of ice the size of a small car and chucked it hard at the dragon. Oscar disappeared and was suddenly cutting at the dragon's face with his miniature rapier. He vanished seconds before the ice Eric had thrown hit the monster in its newly bestowed cuts. To John's surprise, Oscar was suddenly hovering in the air next to them again. He was just marveling at Oscar's speed when Celest stepped forward. Huge fire balls floated menacingly out of a nearby bonfire, and like the snowballs, hurled themselves at the dragon's face. It howled in pain before rushing them. The ice demon had not forgotten that it was Eric who had thrown the first blow. It whipped its long tail around and caused all the bonfires to go out with a single gust of wind, before it began to weave its way toward the ground. It slapped Eric through the side of Terra's home before it took to the sky again to prepare for a fresh attempt.

Celest and John were overcome with anger. They wanted to finish this battle quickly so that they could see if Eric was alright. It was as if an invisible beam of understanding shot between Celest and John. Celest closed her eyes as John flew directly at the dragon. Long streams of glowing embers floated from the piles of smoldering wood that had once been mighty fires. They came to rest in the air between Celest's outstretched hands. The dragon was not going to wait for the little eagle to get to him, and began to advance on John with his fanged mouth wide open. As Celest opened her eyes, the dying embers exploded into a huge fire ball, which she promptly launched not at the dragon, but at John. For an instant in time, it looked as if Celest had just taken out her little brother. Suddenly a loud screeching sound filled the air, and out of the floating inferno John emerged. He was no longer the "little eagle" that the ice dragon was so anxious to devour, but an incredibly large firebird. Its eyes were like molten globes of lava, and instead of feathers it had flames that were all licking the night air with relish. In fact, the only solid parts of the firebird were its white-hot talons. John was now only a quarter of the size of the ice dragon, but the dragon looked slightly unsure of itself all the same. John hovered in the air for a few seconds and filled the village of Rose Brew with shimmering light.

If anyone, not knowing about the battle coming to a climax above, happened to look upon the village as they were passing by, they would think that Rose Brew was one of the most beautiful places in the world. Everything glittered like it was encrusted with diamonds and rubies.

The ice dragon being a proud and vicious creature refused to stand down. It rushed John, who in turn flew directly at it. The monster did not even have time to roar in pain. John had flown straight through it, and was landing even as it was melting. The liquid that the dragon had turned into never touched the ground. It turned into mist and was scattered by the wind. John, now standing in front of his sister and King Oscar, lowered his great flaming head. The warmth he radiated filled Rose Brew and the land around it as he reverted to his eagle form. The once frozen ponds and rivers sprang into motion again. The once dead landscape became as green and alive as the most fertile rain forest. Rose Brew's endless summer had returned.

The Heroes of Rose Brew

When Oscar, Celest, and John went into Terra's home to check on Eric, they found him lying on the couch wrapped in blankets. Terra had already seen to his wounds, and had applied a paste of the same blue leaves that Oscar had once told Celest to suck on for energy. Terra came around the corner and said in a satisfied voice, "Your little brother will be fine. Those leaves I made into an ointment and put on Eric's cuts will supply them with the energy they need to heal." Celest thanked Terra before she and John went upstairs to collapse onto their warm beds. They got some well earned sleep. The siblings must have been very tired, because they seemed too tired to even dream. Oscar did not go to bed, but went outside to talk to Stormy.

Oscar stood on a newly uncovered boulder and smiled at Stormy as he spoke, "Thanks for listening to me and giving the children a chance to fight a battle on their own. They did fine, and I'm sure that they will be up to any challenge they meet. I barely had to help them at all—they're extraordinary!" Stormy pawed at the ground and Oscar seemed to know exactly what was on Stormy's mind. "Only Eric was hurt at all, and his wounds were very minor, he'll be fine. Terra has already seen to his injuries."

When Celest and John awoke the next day, they were anxious to get downstairs and see how everyone was doing. When they got to the kitchen they found Eric happily munching on his toast and strawberry jam. Celest was very relieved to see that all his wounds were already healed. The medicine Terra had applied worked wonders. Terra smiled and told Celest and John to take a seat, and have some breakfast. She handed them little plates with jam and toast on them as she said, "We are having a light breakfast today. We'll need to save room for later!"

At that moment Oscar flew in through the kitchen window and bowed to Terra with a grin on his face, "Everything is set up in the village square."

Terra smiled and nodded as Oscar flew back outside, before turning to the Windheart children and saying, "We are having a party in your honor, and it starts at three o'clock in the square. When you are finished with your breakfast meet me outside. You have never been able to see Rose Brew properly, and it's about time you did!"

As Terra led them around the grounds, Celest and her brothers immediately understood why the village was called Rose Brew. The rivers and the ponds all had the slight smell of rose oil about them. The different colors they saw took their breath away. There were at least a hundred different types of flowers and fruits that covered the land as far as the eye could see. Terra laughed slightly as she pointed to a river that went up and down the humps of twenty hills. She smiled excitedly as she said, "We are going to ride that river to the lake it leads into, and from the lake it is only a little way to the village square. I am so excited; I have not done this for years! If all goes according to plan, we should be there just in time."

As they reached the river they saw a boat carved out of a fallen tree trunk, and it was surrounded by jewel-bright dragonflies. As they all sat down, it became apparent just how fast the river was flowing. Terra laughed nervously as she undid the rope that held them to shore. Suddenly, the scenery became a happy blur as they rushed up and down the hills, splashing each time they reached a valley. Celest, for one, thought that this was better than any water park ride she had ever been on.

When at last they got to the lake they found it was covered in flowers that could possibly be related to our water lilies. The flowers covering each section of the lake came in many colors: reds, blues, greens, and yellows to name a few. The flowers drifted lazily out of their way as their boat headed for shore. Eric was dreamily watching a scarlet humming bird as it stopped to drink the nectar of a nearby green flower when Celest spoke, "Terra, does anyone know all about the plants of Rose Brew? You know, like their names and uses?"

Terra grinned for a moment before she answered, "No, not likely. The plant life here is so diverse that it seems that it would take an eternity to learn them all. Just so you have an idea of what I am saying, think of this, I have been studying the plant life here for a little over six hundred years, and I have barely scratched the surface."

Celest was taken aback, six hundred years had passed and Terra was still learning about Rose Brew's vegetation.

She was still thinking about how many different plants there had to be in order to not know all their names after six hundred years, when a thought occurred to her, "Terra, do all the plants here grow super fast?"

Terra took a moment before answering, "No, less than a quarter of the plants here grow as fast as you saw them do just now. The reason for their sudden appearance is that you and your brothers suddenly broke the ice dragon's spell."

"Oh," she said as she smiled and waved happily to Stormy who was waiting for them on the shore. Just as the boat touched the bank, Celest hopped out and hugged Stormy around the neck. As she let go Celest asked, "Did you hear that we stopped the ice dragon?" Celest gave Stormy a blow by blow account as they started to make their way to the square. When she reached the part of her story where Eric was hurt, Stormy shot Oscar a slightly accusing look. As Oscar had just joined them to keep them company, he looked a little confused.

John must have noticed this because he quickly added, "But thankfully Terra got him taken care of right away!" Celest nodded in agreement and then went on to talk about how she and John just seemed to know that they could join powers, and the powerful fire bird John had turned into with her help.   Oscar smiled at Stormy and said, "Even if you were given all the time in the world, you would not have enough to find a closer set of siblings."

Celest and John both asked at the same time, "What does our being close have to do with what happened last night?"

Oscar chuckled a little before he answered, "You *are*

close. While the blood you share gives you the ability to combine your powers, it is your closeness that lets you do it so well. In addition, it was your closeness that let you simply *know* about that particular gift."

As the happy group stepped into the village square they were slightly overwhelmed by the loud cheering that erupted all around them. The only part still left of the gazebo that once covered the square, was its marble pillars. The pillars still stood at the corners of the square, but now they were tightly wrapped in a variety of flowering vines. The air was full of confetti, and all the trees had colorful streamers hanging from them. Aside from the great food there was also entertainment. An elfin band played a lively tune as dancing elfin women twirled across the dance floor with their silken dresses billowing out around them. There were also jugglers tossing flaming broadswords high into the air and doing a series of cartwheels before catching them and sending them skyward again. And as the sun began to set, the elves began to shoot off fire works. Celest and her brothers were watching the different shapes that the fire works were taking in the sky with great interest. The different patterns included hearts, stars, and to the Windhearts' surprise, large and detailed fiery portraits of themselves. John was just wondering exactly how they got the sparks to go where they were needed to make the pictures, when Oscar came floating up to them with Stormy at his heals.

Oscar seemed to be very pleased about something as he said, "The unveiling is about to take place. Stormy agrees with me that this is something that you really should see!" Celest hopped off of the stool she had been sitting on and took Eric by the hand.

As John hopped onto Celest's shoulder he asked, "What is it that you guys are showing us?"

Oscar smiled and said, "As much as I'd love to tell you...I am afraid that it is a surprise." Stormy and Oscar lead them into the very center of the village square where there was a huge something draped in a huge tarp.

Terra was waiting for them when they arrived. "You are going to love this!" she said with a grin as dazzling as the starlight that they were bathed in.

Anticipation filled the air as a drum roll began, and the elves started to chant the numbers of the count down in unison. "Five!" Six golden fireworks shot into the air. "Four!" Seven silver fireworks did the same. "Three!" Eight deep red fireworks followed suit. "Two!" Nine bright blue fireworks kissed the sky. "One!" It seemed like no less than a hundred fireworks shot high into the sky. It looked like every color in existence filled the night sky. Terra ran forward and pulled a long red silk rope. Seconds later the tarp fell to the ground revealing a huge golden fountain which immediately sprang to life. It depicted the Windhearts: John was suspended on a thick crystal pipe. Not only did the pipe supply him the water that now flowed off his back and wings, but it was so clear that it really looked as if he was flying. Celest was holding her hands skyward. The water was timed so that great balls of water shot out from between them, which somehow looked like the fireballs Celest had launched at the ice dragon. Eric was holding a large block of crystal, which gleamed like an iceberg above his head. The water flowed from the top of it, creating a thin wall of water all around him. Celest looked around at the sea of smiling faces surrounding her and her brothers. Overcome with emotion at such a wonderful gesture, her vision was becoming blurred with tears. The Windhearts did not feel that they had said thank you enough, although they must have said it more than fifty times.

A tall black elf with silvery gray eyes walked up and shook Celest's hand as he said, "You did a magnificent job! Perhaps your fates are not as doomed to darkness as we once thought. No one truly believed that the ice dragon could be defeated by children. We wish you luck. Your next adversary is much more powerful than the ice dragon and it does not approve of the slaying of any of his fellows. But still, you've beaten similar odds." Oscar nodded as Terra told the crowd that it was now time to let the Windhearts get some rest. She turned to Celest's group and nodded for them to follow her home. As soon as they got there, Terra went and got Celest and Oscar some fresh green silk pajamas.

She chuckled merrily as she spoke, "You see, the village of Rose Brew is very much indebted to you. What's more is that they know it. You will always have a home here, you have but to ask. Money is not a factor in this village. Even if it were, I very much doubt that anyone here would accept it from you—the heroes of Rose Brew. Now, I was informed by Oscar that you will be leaving the day after tomorrow. I will finish getting the supplies ready before I go to sleep, which I will go over with you after breakfast tomorrow. But in the mean time sleep well."

FROM NIGHTMARE TO
MIDNIGHT DREAM

Celest was riding a golden tree over the edge of a waterfall when the tree took flight. The sky was painted with rainbows as she soared high above the world. The sun was tucked away in a fluffy blanket of reds and oranges. Everything in her life today was soothing. As Celest passed through a cloud, it cooled her face with a light mist. Out of nowhere, the once sweet and tame clouds became vicious as rabid dogs. The healing light that had once surrounded her turned into heavy darkness. Suddenly she was being chased by a midnight black, shapeless mass of darkness. The only features she could make out were its burning white eyes and its ebony claws that gleamed in the little twilight that seemed to be left in the world. Celest urged her tree to go faster but it refused. The creature was gaining. Just when she felt as if all hope were gone she looked to see a nearby storm cloud turn into Stormy. The great thunder horse flew between her and the pursuing monster and pumped his great wings forcing the creature back. Celest turned around to help Stormy. She put both of her hands in front of her and a great whirlwind added itself to Stormy's attack and helped push the creature farther back still. Suddenly she was listening to the end of Mrs. Windheart's story. When she looked at her four year old self, she had the strangest feeling that her younger self could see her too. Strangely enough, it was as comforting as it was unnerving. Celest was just about to speak to the wide-eyed little girl when she woke up. And when she awoke she could not even remember what it was she was about to ask.

When Celest and her brothers got downstairs, Terra had already made breakfast as usual. Today's breakfast included honey glazed ham, eggs, pancakes, and fluffy biscuits covered in a sausage gravy. This morning it was cold chocolate milk to drink. Celest was frowning slightly as she poked at a biscuit.

As she put a forkful in her mouth John asked her, "What's wrong? I thought you liked biscuits and gravy."

Celest was brought out of her stupor by John's question. She turned to him and asked, "Since we have been in this world, what have your dreams been like?"

John shrugged and replied, "The same as my dreams have always been. Only instead of darkness, I get to see. Why?"

Celest took a little time to think by taking a swig of chocolate milk. After a moment she answered, "My dreams have been a little different here. Do you remember that dream I use to have all the time? The one I always had after Dad had been gone for a while?"

John's eyes seemed to be looking into a past that he could not see. Even with his special gifts. When John came out of his reverie he said, "Dad was always in and out of our lives, mostly out. Yup, I think I know the one you're talking about, the one where you're asking Mom about him?"

Celest nodded as she went on, "Well, since we have been here, I have been having that dream more often than not. Even though I am pretty sure that what I am about to tell you is just happening because of the danger we have been facing here, it still creeps me out. Now there is some sort of monster that is trying to get me...and sometimes Mom too. I can never completely make it out. All I get are glimpses of it. Its glowing eyes are completely white when I see them. Other times all I can see is...a shadowy wing...dark razor sharp claws, but I never get to see the complete picture. Its like someone...someone is hiding it from me." Oscar had been listening while sipping his coffee. Something seemed to tighten within his gentle features. No one noticed that Oscar had stood up and left through the kitchen window while John was telling Celest in a slightly horror-struck voice that he was sure that it was nothing to be worried about.

While the Windheart children were enjoying their breakfast, Oscar was to be found on the once icy tree stump that Stormy had nearly nudged John off of. He was adamantly talking to Stormy. His eyebrows were narrowed so close together as he spoke that it looked like he had a tiny furry caterpillar crawling across his forehead, "The dark king seems to have found a way to harass Celest by invading her dreams! I do not know what to do! I can help protect her physically but her dreams are out of my reach.

I can't protect her there at all." Stormy gazed deeply into Oscar's eyes for a moment before turning away and heading to Terra's house. Oscar called after him as he followed, "I *know* that she has strength running through her veins. I also know that she is a lot stronger than anyone gives her credit for being, but do not forget that she is still a child! We can't just let her face these dreams on her own!"

As Stormy and Oscar reached Terra's front door it opened. Eric came rushing out and did a front hand spring before landing gracefully on Stormy's back. John and Celest both said good morning as Terra came out behind them. Terra waved for everyone to follow her around the back of her house. Once everyone got there she waited for their attention before she spoke, "I have already prepared the traveling packs in which I have put both food and medicinal herbs to help make this a safer journey. This is a getveable root." Terra held up what looked like a silver carrot with golden leaves shaped like stars. "Its purpose is to draw out poisons; it works well against most venom. These," she now held up a massive clump of the blue leaves Celest had seen used on two occasions, "are lightning leaves. Their use is to give a large boost of energy. The more used, the greater the effect. They are useful in a lot of different situations, every thing from just getting through a day that's dragging horribly, to giving the body a swift kick into overdrive to speed up the healing process. You'll be happy to hear that lightning leaves have no side effects whatsoever. Those are the main ones we might need. If you have any questions about the other herbs at anytime just ask. Also, I have put in a variety of—" Oscar gave her an apologetic look as he cut her off.

"*We might need?* Are you saying that you are coming

with us? There are two things that make me think you shouldn't. One, we could not possibly ask you to face the danger we are surely going to have to. And two, while Stormy is a big fellow, I doubt that there would be enough room on his back for you to ride with us in any comfort."

Terra's face looked resolute as she softly replied, "There is no need to ask me for anything, I've already made up my mind. The Windhearts are good kids who deserve all the help they can get. And as to the travel arrangements, I have a large enclosed glider, which I could attach to the harness I already have fashioned for Stormy to wear, with Stormy's permission of course." Stormy looked at Terra appraisingly before nodding his consent. Terra's face broke into a wide grin as she said, "Now as I was saying earlier, I have put in a variety of drinks, soups, and sandwiches in special jars that keep everything that is supposed to be cold, ice cold. And anything that is better served hot will be kept at the appropriate temperature as long as it is needed to be. Thank you, Stormy, I am already very attached to these children. I feel that I need to see them through to the very end."

The rest of the day passed as smoothly and steadily as a gentle stream making its way to a great river. They passed the day playing cards, and talking about what they thought this new monster might be capable of.

The next day everyone was up long before the sun was. For a morning snack Terra had made everyone a hot pie filled with a transparent fruit that tasted like a combination of apples and cool kiwi ice cream. She put on her own travel pack, handed one to Celest, a tiny one to Oscar, and a very large one to Eric. Before the Windhearts knew it, they were soaring high in the sky following a long curving river that seemed to go on forever. The night before, Terra had told them that if they followed the Midnight Dream River, it would lead them to their next destination. She also added before hopping into her glider that the ruined city of Tionaughty, which their next adversary was responsible for destroying more than a hundred years ago, could only be accessed in the twilit hours of dusk and dawn. Celest was laying on her stomach looking at the river below. It glowed bright green and gold because of the hundreds of fireflies that all seemed to live there.

John was on his back staring into the still star strewn sky. Celest looked at him and said, "I thought I asked you to stop laying like that. You are an eagle in this world, and birds only lay like that when they are not alive anymore! It…bothers me."

John looked at his sister warmly as he spoke, "It is just comfortable to me. I was human a lot longer than I've been an eagle, but…if it bothers you, I'll stop."

Celest smiled and said sleepily, "Thanks, but you're right. I think I am just being weird."

Eric was only awake long enough to gobble down his breakfast which included hot maple porridge and toast. The moment Eric and his brother and sister were done eating he went back to sleep. Celest and John could not simply go back to sleep like their little brother, so they spent the day talking about Celest's dreams, practicing, and playing cards with Terra and Oscar inside the glider. Whenever Celest told John about a particularly scary part of her nighttime journeys through the ever-changing dreamscape, John would say in uneasy tones, "It's probably nothing to worry about." Although Celest noticed that he seemed to be saying this to himself as much as he was saying it to her, she never let on that she knew how worried John was. She seemed to think that it would only make him worry more.

To train, Celest would turn masses of clouds into the shapes of animals from their world while John would try to guess which animal was which. It was a real challenge for John. As he had never *seen* any of the animals himself, he had to try to remember details of what he was told they looked like. He did surprisingly well.

A few hours passed with the cloud game in full swing before John took to the sky and did a lot of tricks. One of Oscar's favorites was when John flew around Stormy's head so fast that he looked like a golden blur. One of John's feathers must have brushed against Stormy's nose. Because out of nowhere, Stormy sneezed so hard that John tumbled at least a mile through the air ahead of them. John laughed uncontrollably as he flew back to land on Stormy's head. After the laughter had subsided, Celest and John taught Oscar and Terra how to play rummy. While both Terra and Oscar were fast learners, it was Terra who mopped the floor with everyone else. John smiled as he said, "Beginner's luck!"

Oscar laughed a little as he added, "Then why couldn't I have had some?"

The Ruins of Tionaughty

It was a little after seven o'clock when Oscar called back from Stormy's head that they were about to land. Stormy landed beside the river with a soft thud. John looked up and noticed that the sun was nearing the end of its daily ride across the sky. Celest looked out at the huge clearing that stretched for countless miles in front of them. For some strange reason it gave her the chills. After a few moments she whispered in the same manner that someone would adopt while kneeling beside a dying person's bed, "Why is the air so heavy here?"

Terra answered as she hopped out of her glider. "The air pressure changes when it nears the changing time. Some say that the air is mourning the loss of lives at the hands of the Tionaughty beast." As the sun crept just beyond the horizon, it happened in an instant. The ruins of a once great city blossomed in the twilight, appearing out of thin air to fill the forest clearing. Oscar and Terra led the way and Stormy brought up the rear. As

Stormy stepped across the city's border, the night finished establishing itself. They watched in disbelief as the world around them vanished and was engulfed in total darkness. Celest turned away from the unsettling scene with a sense of foreboding before pressing on with the others. As they walked they saw tiny flecks of twilight following them. The fleeting dance of darkness and light quickly moved from one pile of crumbled building to the next. Celest had an uncomfortable feeling that these flecks of twilight were very similar to the shadows that had followed them through the JaPoyPoy forest.

When she told Oscar her concerns he smiled and said, "Maybe you share some of John's sight abilities. Humans usually cannot see the hidden ones." Eric, who had been following one of the light specs, slid back to Celest's side as Oscar chuckled and nodded toward him. "Like you, Eric also seems to share this gift." Eric gave Oscar a slightly reproachful look. "Most of the shadow folk are harmless, just curious. Some however, are spies for the dark king."

Celest looked at her brothers and asked, "Is it normal for us to share some of our powers?"

Oscar laughed, "You and your brothers are far from 'normal.' You are so close that the abilities you all have, spill into each other. Due to Eric, you and John are slightly stronger than you would normally be. Because of you, John and Eric have a slightly stronger resistance to the elements. And as you have learned with the fire bird, when you use your abilities together they grow much stronger."

As John looked around, he worried slightly. How on earth would they be able to defeat something that had all but flattened such a vast city? As they approached the heart of Tionaughty a putrid smell filled the air. The ground in front of them cracked open as shadowy ooze bubbled forth. Oscar drew his sword as Celest's cloak billowed out behind her. Its royal blue seemed to glow in the twilight. John took to the sky, his golden eyes fierce. Eric picked up a nearby tree that had been petrified by time and tapped it lightly against his shoulder. The black slime writhed and began to shape itself into a very solid jackal. The dark beast stood fifteen feet tall, and had bits of moonlight scattered throughout his body. The dark jackal's mouth dripped with saliva and its breath smelled like something had crawled into its mouth and died.

Eric charged the creature and bashed its leg with his club. It howled in anger and crushed the stone tree in one bite. The beast picked Eric up and was just about to bite him in half, when Oscar moved with such speed that it looked as if twenty Oscars had appeared and they all slashed at his front leg at once. It dropped Eric, who somehow managed to land on his feet. The wounds on the dark jackal's foreleg oozed for a moment before they rapidly healed. Celest caused two ruined buildings to soar through the air and crush the monster from both sides, pinching it in half. The jackal looked stunned, and for a moment it seemed as if they had won. The corners of the beast's mouth curled up in a wicked smile. Its front half walked backwards and oozed together with the back. He then turned and rushed the Windheart children with blinding speed. It was just about to snatch Eric up when John raked its face with his razor sharp talons. While the jackal did not seem to be too bothered by this, it did seem to get its attention. It leapt high into the air and was inches from John when it was driven back to the ground in a flash of blue light. Stormy looked furious, he had just pummeled the beast with countless bolts of lightning. It lay on the ground smoldering.

As it slowly got to its feet, Celest pointed at it and wind lashed out in such a focused gust that it was as if dozens of invisible swords diced it into tiny chunks. The little pieces turned into miniature versions of the jackal. Celest looked at the ground and sixty diamonds came bursting out. Her eyes narrowed as she willed them to become hollow. The diamonds then began to absorb the tiny jackals. The little blobs threw themselves violently against the insides of the gems. Celest pointed to her left, her eyes still on the now trapped monsters. Two rocks floated into the air and bashed into each other so hard that they sparked. The spark they created grew into an inferno that engulfed the diamonds. The dark blobs became still as they solidified. The now black diamonds fell to the ground.

As they stood there, the wind began to pick up. Oscar looked from the diamonds to Celest and said, "Well, that's another servant that we don't have to worry about any more. Come on." Oscar and Terra began to leave when Terra froze, her horrorstruck gaze fixed on the sky behind them. Celest slowly turned around. What she saw made her feel as if her heart had dropped into her stomach. There was a great pulsating mass of darkness with white gleaming orbs for eyes coming over the horizon. It was rapidly closing on them.

Oscar flew to sit on Stormy's neck as he yelled, "Terra, get the kids to safety! It's the Oblivion King...they're not ready yet!" Stormy seemed to grow with fury as he made straight for the dark king. John, who was sitting on

Celest's shoulder, had to hold on for dear life when Terra grabbed Eric and Celest's hands and took off running.

Celest held a stitch in her side as she gasped, "What about Stormy and Oscar?"

Terra did not stop to answer, "They are trying to buy us some time. They will get away themselves once they feel that we have gotten the best head start possible."

Apparently the king was too powerful to be held off for long. It was closing in on them. Terra took a sudden sharp turn down an alley, losing the king for a moment. After taking three deep breaths she said, "Get into Eric's bag, now!"

Celest looked puzzled but opened the bag. When she put her head inside her mouth fell open. It was like a large storehouse full of hundreds of herbs and meals. With her head still in the bag she waved for John and Eric to follow. Then she climbed in.

Terra put her head into the bag and said, "Do not come out until one of us gets you. I am going to distract it." Celest and her brothers shook their heads. They were afraid of losing her. Terra smiled and said not to worry before closing the bag and hiding it behind some trash cans. After she covered it with a bunch of dead leaves, she bolted out of the alley and turned right. A deep howling filled the air as a rush of darkness followed her.

The Windhearts sat in tense silence, trying to hear the world beyond the pack's flap. Each one was wondering what was happening to Terra, and what had become of Stormy and Oscar. After a few moments Celest decided that they could do with a distraction, something to get their minds off things while they waited. She got up and looked around for something they could eat. It was not until she found a jar of hot chocolate and a container of roast beef sandwiches, that she realized that they had not eaten since that morning. Celest brought the food out to her brothers along with some coffee mugs she had found. Eric for one was very happy to see the food. John on the other hand looked at the hot meal only for an instant before turning his attention back to the closed doorway above them.

Celest put his plate and drink in front of him as she said, "Not eating will not help anything. If anything, it will make things worse. Think. What if they need our help and we are too weak from hunger to do anything about it." Reluctantly, John tore his gaze away from the exit and began to eat. Eric practically inhaled his food before curling up into a ball, and falling fast asleep. As Celest waited, hours passed, and her eyes grew heavy.

She once again found herself in the room. This time, however, Celest and her younger self were alone. Celest looked around the room before speaking, "Where is Mom?"

The little girl smiled, "She has already gone to bed. Who are you?"

Celest was on the verge of saying "You." But instead she replied, "Just a friend. Tell me, why do you always want to know about your dad? He only has been in your life a few times."

The little girl's eyes sparkled in a way that seemed to say that the answer was very obvious. "He's my dad, knowing where I come from tells me about who I am, and what I can become."

Celest swallowed hard and as she sat down on her bed

she said, "Who your parents are does not determine who you will become…"

The little girl walked up to her and put a hand on each of Celest's knees. Leaning close to her face she smiled as she said, "True, it does not seal your fate in stone. But our parents *are* a part of us. Now you must wake up!"

Celest's eyes snapped open as she heard Terra's voice, "Children, you must wake up! We have got to get going. The dark king has disappeared. But we don't know for how long or if it is just a trap to lure you out. Either way we have got to go!" As Celest looked up she saw that Terra's kind face was sporting a deep cut on her left cheek. Celest woke Eric and John up. John flew out of the bag, and Eric flipped up the ladder with ease. Celest came out last and threw her arms around Terra. Eric did likewise. John, however, perched himself on the side of a trashcan looking very sad.

Celest noticed and called to him, "Why don't you come over here and join the group hug? You're just as happy to see Terra as we are."

John's eyes were slightly watery as he took a silent pause before saying, "Can't, no arms." Terra patted Celest and Eric on the back a few times before walking up to swoop John into her arms.

Terra smiled warmly as she said, "Come on, it is nearly dawn and we still need to find Oscar and Stormy." After walking a few blocks they found Stormy trotting up to them with a hurt Oscar laying on his back. Celest and her brother rushed to see if Oscar was alright.

"What happened?" Celest asked Oscar as she approached.

Oscar laughed, "Unlike Stormy here, I do not have the

luxury of letting harm pass through me. I was knocked to the ground as Stormy held him off. The Oblivion King was furious. The dark king could not hurt him. All his attacks just went straight through. Stormy's attacks on the other hand…well, let us just say that the evil king had to dodge around Stormy to come after you. Remember when I told you how the king wishes to harm Stormy's children due to their being powerful creatures? The reason is that a storm cannot be hurt or controlled. Only the son of He who made all things could ever control a storm with a word."

Everyone in the group seemed to be very happy to be together again. Together they made their way back to the entrance of Tionaughty. Oscar gave a tired sigh before saying, "The crossing time is now, dawn." The world around the city seemed to blossom from the darkness. Stormy, Oscar, and Terra had just passed the city limits when the now too familiar deep howling filled the air. The Windhearts began to run as the Oblivion King appeared on the horizon. The monster was almost instantly upon them. Just as the children were about to cross the border, Eric tripped. Huge jaws emerged from the darkness surrounding the king ready to snatch him up. Celest ran back to save him. As she raised her fists into the air in front of her, an eight foot thick granite wall exploded from the ground to stand between Eric and the king. As Celest grabbed Eric's hand the granite wall began to crumble. The two leaped over the border as the city vanished. The Oblivion King was sealed inside, at least until dusk. After a few moments their heart rates returned to normal and they prepared to leave. Before long, the little group of heroes were on their way back to Bulaklak Haven.

Oscar held his hand out in front of him and a tiny ball of golden light shot out ahead of them and disappeared into the horizon. He then flew back into one of the windows of Terra's glider, and with a satisfied smile on his face he told her, "I have just sent an order requesting that a house be built next to the Windhearts'. It will be very comfortable and should suit all your needs nicely." Terra thanked him and they passed the time until their arrival playing rummy.

THE DARK KNIGHT

Upon their arrival, loud horns greeted them with enthusiasm. Terra's house was as nice as the one that was built for the Windhearts. It too was decorated with flowery stained glass windows. Terra was very impressed, and she told Oscar how wonderful she thought his kingdom was. He thanked her and said, "I am happy you like it. If there is anything you want while you are here, just ask. I have told my people to treat your requests with the same respect that they would mine. I don't know if it would interest you, but we have an excellent garden which includes some of the rarer varieties of fruits, herbs, and vegetables. We even have our own crop of kaholoholo melons. It would be my pleasure to show it to you sometime if you like."

Terra smiled and said, "Yes, please. I would love to see the garden." Oscar grinned and said that he had to go and tell Marlene how everyone was doing, and he also informed them that their houses had already been stocked with all the comforts needed to make a home. As he left for his castle he called back to them that lunch would be served in the courtyard and they would discuss their next course of action then.

The next day came as quickly as quick silver rolling down a steep glass hill. Before anyone had time to grasp and enjoy the night, day was upon them and then lunch. Oscar had set before them the usual smorgasbord. It was a rich combination of the food belonging to the world that they currently inhabited, and a subtle array of the Windhearts' favorite foods. Everyone was happily chatting about their recent adventures. Oscar was just telling Marlene how Celest and John had managed to crush the ice dragon when a woebegone fairy soldier landed beside the table and kneeled looking at the ground in front of him.

Oscar looked at the young man's scuffed armor with the gravest of expressions as the soldier spoke, "Sir, Oblivion King has sent a small army of his ratadda warriors. They march on the kingdom even as we speak. We are doing all we can to hold them at bay. But, our powers seem to be having little to no effect. Also, the fact that their powers feel miniscule compared to the one who commands them from the rear seems to suggest that we are doomed, sir."

Celest looked at Oscar and asked, "Who are these ratadda warriors?"

He looked into Celest's deep brown eyes and answered, "The ratadda are a race of barbarians. Other than their boar heads and excessively thick hairy arms they have human bodies. They are so power hungry that they decided to follow the Oblivion King just to sip on the dregs of his dark might. The problem that my folk have with them is that they are all but impervious to our powers, fairy powers that is. You see, they have a high resistance to 'wild' energies. I wanted you to have at least a little break from your hard journey before we moved on. I regret to have to ask you to postpone this resting time in order to ensure the safety of my kingdom once more. Please, will you help my kingdom?"

John laughed and said, "Oscar, you have done so much for us that there is no way in *either* world that we would say no." Celest nodded and Eric belched. Celest and John looked at their little brother for a moment and he laughed. Oscar and Terra could not help but to laugh as well. Stormy did not laugh but whinnied and nodded his majestic head. After Celest had downed the last of her zana, they made their way to the battle field three miles north of Bulaklak Haven.

In the distance they could see the monsters that now threatened Oscar's kingdom. Their armor was black with the filth of years. It was clear that the ratadda did not care much for cleanliness. Oscar called to his knights, in a surprisingly booming voice for such a tiny person, that it was time for them to return to their homes and to tend to the wounded. With Oscar's army gone, it was six against six hundred. If you did not know what the Windhearts and their companions were capable of, one might say that they faced impossible odds. For this group however, impossible was a word that seemed never to apply.

A deep grunting voice echoed from the rear flank of the ratadda army. Although no one could understand the language that was spoken, the meaning was very clear. At the voice's word, the ratadda warriors drew their bows and sent an ominous cloud of arrows in their direction. Celest was just about to create a protective wall of some sort when John flew high above them. As he gave a loud skreegh, a golden light surrounded his body, and then it surrounded the whole group in the form of a huge golden sphere. As the arrows collided with it they turned into a golden glitter and floated harmlessly to the ground.

Oscar smiled brightly, "As I once said, 'the golden eagles of this realm are incredibly powerful creatures by their own right' and he is definitely no ordinary golden eagle."

High above, John was staring at the ratadda's commander. He was a frightening knight. His armor was not black with filth, but was highly polished ebony. He stood as tall as the dark jackal, and his midnight-black cape drifted gently on a breeze behind him. He plunged his twelve foot, black broad sword into the earth beside him. At his command one of his subordinates tossed him a huge crossbow, and a long black arrow. John watched the darkness-knight as he loaded the deadly bolt and aimed at him. Although the knight was at least four miles away, John's sight allowed him to see the knight as though he was standing right in front of him.

Just as the villain took aim and delivered his lethal attack, John saw passed the armor and yelled, "No! Stop! You have no idea what you are doing! You're being controlled!" But it was too late. The arrow flew through the air leaving a trail of inky darkness behind it. It did not deteriorate as the other arrows did, but easily penetrated the golden barrier and tore through the flesh between John's right wing and his chest. He fell to the ground in a crumpled ball. John was trying with all his might to tell everyone that it was not his fault, that the knight was being controlled. But Eric had already tossed Celest onto his back and was running with such force that his super strong legs left large craters in the ground with every stride. Thunder filled the air as Oscar mounted Stormy's neck, and they too went after the vile scum that had so badly hurt John.

As they left, Oscar called back to Terra saying, "Get John back to the kingdom, and do all you can for him." As everyone disappeared from sight, John tried to tell Terra what he had seen. Terra could not understand a single word he was saying; all she could hear was John's weak mumbling. He continued to try until the darkness took him.

Three days passed before Celest and the others returned. When they arrived at the Windhearts' house, they found Terra fast asleep next to John's bed. As she woke up, Celest noticed that her eyes were red and puffy. Apparently she had cried herself to sleep. She looked desperately from Eric, to Oscar, to Celest and her voice broke slightly as she spoke, "I don't know if he will make it. He has lost so much blood. Normally my folk can tell. We have a unique sense when it comes to animals. But for some reason I just can't tell! I just can't tell…"

Oscar looked at Terra with a sad kindness in his eyes and said, "You've done your part. You dressed his wound, and made him as comfortable as you could. The reason that you can't tell if he will pull through or not is because he is not an ordinary animal, he is a golden eagle and yet he is not. Please try to get some rest. I can have a bottle of our finest wine sent to your house if you like. It might help you get some sleep." Terra declined the wine, but went to her house. Celest could not hear anything that was going on around her. There was a horrible ringing in her ears, and when she heard that John might die she felt as if a professional boxer had punched her in her stomach with all his might. Oscar told Celest in a gentle voice that it was not her fault.

But Celest snapped at him and said, "You don't have a clue what you're talking about. If I was just a little faster putting up a wall to protect us John would be alright!" Celest felt a surge of guilt for shouting at Oscar. She knew that he was only trying to comfort her. "I'm sorry, I just don't know what to do."

Oscar shook his head, "I understand. You're under a lot of stress right now. John is strong. I am sure he'll pull through."

Celest kneeled tiredly beside John's bed and said, "Please, don't give up on me. Me, Eric and Mom need you." She then promptly fell asleep with her head next to John's now bandaged body. As Celest tumbled through darkness and into a deep sleep, she heard voices behind her.

Oscar was talking to Marlene, "Celest and Stormy scattered the entire army trying to get at that knight. It looked like they had him, but as they closed in on him he simply turned and walked into the shadow of an oak tree. God knows where he came out. He is a shadow walker. You know, step into one shadow and instantly step out of any other shadow he chooses…" Celest felt a fresh wave of anger at the knight's escape. But suddenly she saw John stumbling through the darkness in the distance. He was in his human form.

Celest rushed to his side and put a hand on his shoulder and said, "John? Are you alright?" John turned to her, tears streaming from his tightly closed eyes, "Celest! I'm so happy to hear your voice one last time. For some reason my sight has left me again. And a scary voice has been telling me that I will die soon and I will never see you or any one else I love again."

Celest looked wary as she watched John sobbing and asked sharply, "Where is this voice coming from? Can you tell me what direction?" John pointed and Celest was surprised to hear an eagle cry in the opposite direction. Gathering her resolve she said, "Did you hear that eagle?" John nodded. "Follow its call. I am sure it will lead you out of here. I have something that I have to deal with first, but don't worry, I'm always behind you." Celest stood for a moment watching John stumble after the eagle's voice, before facing the solid darkness behind her, "Oblivion King!"

To her shock the darkness around her shifted itself as a voice surrounded her, "Not quite, I am the taint and true power behind the black arrow…darkness eternal."

Celest stood tall and with her head held high said, "Listen to me monster. Come near anyone I care about again and I will put that 'eternal' part of your name to the ultimate test, got me? And deliver that message to the dark king for me once you get out of my brother and let him heal properly." Celest turned on her heel and slowly walked away, not remotely afraid. The dark king had just trodden on forbidden territory by hurting a loved one so badly. As she walked away she felt her conscious self awaken. Once her eyes were opened she was pleasantly surprised to see John's eyes opening.

John looked at her and croaked, "Thanks, Celest. That

knight, he is really an elfin teenager. It's not his fault. He's trapped in that evil armor's chest while a monster in the right shoulder force feeds him darkness." And with out further comment he fell back asleep, this time a peaceful one.

They stayed in Bulaklak Haven for another two weeks. The time was meant to both give John a chance to finish healing, and to give the Windhearts a chance to rest. The Windhearts spent much of their time outdoors; Oscar had shown them a huge waterfall eight miles west of the kingdom. He told the children that this was the water-fall that fed the lake that Stormy had taken Celest to. It was a magnificent sight. It was at least one thousand and fifty feet tall. The waterfall was made up of two parts. The main flow of falling water formed an eighty foot wide curtain of pure rushing power. The second part of the falls was composed of eight smaller waterfalls. The little water falls seemed to resonate with different colors as they leapt from rock to rock. Terra said that this was probably due to the tiny crystals coloring the rocks.

Oscar confirmed this, "Precisely, all the rocks forming this cliff are an ore belonging to one type of gem or another. Sunset will be here in an hour or so. We will wait until then before we go back. The sunset sets these falls on fire with different colored lights." Celest was recounting what John had told her about the ebony armored leader of the ratadda to Terra, when John felt his insides squirm. He had not even told Celest what had bothered him the most about the encounter. Well, other than being pierced through with a monstrous arrow. The boy was a young teenager, and he had both Terra's eyes and skin tone. The only difference between his eyes and Terra's, was that her eyes were always full of gentle warmth. The boy's, on the other hand, were blank and filled with an indescribable anger. John did not know if he should let Terra know or not. He felt that it would be cruel to get her hopes up only for it to not be her son at all, or even worse, for it to be her son and not being able to save him. John was still contemplating his dilemma when the last rays of daylight hit the water fall, and his fears gave into awe. Oscar was not exaggerating; both the waterfalls and the cliff they tumbled over were illuminated with brilliant shades of ruby, sapphire, emerald and countless other gem colors.

It was on their last day before their departure that John asked Oscar, "Where to next?"

Oscar was watching Eric do acrobatics. He turned saying, "We need to seek the rings of Aquados, as our next destination rests beneath the sea. Unfortunately, the only one on land who has these is the oldest dragon in the world. His name is Iron-Back."

Celest asked Oscar in a curious voice, "What do the rings of Aquados do? And aren't dragons…bad?"

Oscar laughed, "While I do not like dragons in general due to their nasty habit of eating other creatures alive, it is never wise to stereotype. I actually hear that Iron-Back is a good natured dragon. So, while I do not want you to stereotype him as an evil creature, stay on your guard because it is in his nature to eat other living creatures. Oh, and the rings of Aquados allow you to function under water in the same ways you would on land, or in the air," Oscar added with a little bow to John.

CELEST'S CHALLENGE

The next day, Celest and her brothers woke up early to prepare for their upcoming journey. Before even Terra and Oscar were awake, they had asked some of Oscar's subjects to help them gather supplies. Celest stepped into the different bags and did an inventory. With John's help she told the fairies what they needed. And with Eric's help they loaded crate after crate into the bags. John told Celest that he was going to take Eric and go to tell Stormy what they were going to do, and who they needed to get the rings from to do it.

As she watched John fly off with Eric following on the ground, Celest heard Oscar's voice behind her, "Very impressive, you and your brothers have prepared for our trip with out any assistance from us. Such initiative! Now, I need you to take a walk with me. I've already asked Terra to let everyone know where we have gone to. Once the timing is right."

Oscar led Celest back to the waterfall they had visited

earlier not speaking a word as they went. It looked like he was questioning his own actions. Celest noticed, and hoped that she would be able to help him sort out whatever was weighing on his mind. As Celest took her seat on a rock near the falls, Oscar stared at the misting base of the waterfall. As though taking resolve from the beautiful display of power he slowly began to speak, "Drifting on the seas of pure nothingness. Scattered just beyond the shore of memories, sleeps a legend which concerns you. At least I think it does. Those of my bloodline have been keeping the secret of what you are about to hear for many millennia. When the dark one was sealed away long, long ago my ancestors along with the dwarfs of Auration Mountain forged a tool. This tool was made to focus the powers of a great champion who would do battle with the dark one once he managed to break free of his prison. The item spoken of in this legend would accept only the one worthy of its power. It is said that there would be only one who would wield it to its full potential, and that it would reject all others who tried to claim its properties for their own uses. My great, great, great grandmother knew that there were beings who felt that if they could not have its power they would not allow anyone else to. Even if it meant that they had to destroy it themselves. She took the tool and sealed it away in a space folded in time. The key to this space is my crown. When I told Stormy that I thought you were the one spoken of he did not want me to tell you. You see, if you are not the one, you could very well die trying to get it. You would be tested severely. It is no task for the faint of heart, but as you have proven yourself many times over…I just felt that you have the right to know."

Celest sat in silence for a moment before she spoke, "Thank you for telling me. I think that we will need any advantage we can get against the Oblivion King. I would like to try. If something happens to me please tell my brothers and my mom that I love them and tell Stormy and Terra that I will always be grateful for their friendship. And very importantly, thank you, Oscar. You are a good friend." Oscar's eyes filled with tears as he took off his crown and held it above his head. A portal opened in thin air.

Oscar flew up to Celest and handed her his crown, "Once you have done what you feel you must, hold my crown and think of those you love. It will bring you back into our regular time, our regular world." Stormy and the others were just arriving as Celest was stepping into the portal, she paused to wave goodbye before continuing on. Stormy looked at Oscar with eyes so hard that they could have easily cut diamond. But after a moment, they filled with despair as he nervously pawed at the ground. Eventually, he let out a frustrated snort and lay on the cool earth to await Celest's return. John and Eric leaned against him and closed their eyes.

Terra stood beside Oscar and whispered, "It will be alright. I believe with all my heart that she will make it out alright."

Celest came out beside the waterfall. The only differences she could see so far was that the water was flowing up the cliff face instead of down, and that now there was a rotting wooden door beside the base leading into the rock wall. Swallowing hard she pushed the door open and stepped inside. It was like a forgotten castle. The only light was coming from the glowing fungus that was growing on the gray stone walls. The air felt so thin that Celest found herself breathing faster than usual. As she proceeded down the great hallway she wondered if she had made the right decision. She could not help but wonder if her family would be all right without her.

As she pressed on, she heard a woman's voice fill the hallway, "To defeat your foe you must know your foe. To understand your foe you must first know yourself." Trying to see where the voice had come from she slowed her pace but never stopped walking.

After she passed a rusted suit of armor, she found another wooden door. This one was not rotting away like the other. In fact it seemed that not even dust could cling to it. Once she pulled it open she found a room that seemed to be carved out of a smooth red crystal. After she stepped inside, the door slammed shut behind her. Looking around the room she saw two crystal barrels full of water with red and yellow rose petals floating on the surface. At the far end of the chamber she found a golden box.

As Celest approached it, the voice she had heard earlier filled the room, "It is never wise to make assumptions, so it would be wise to always think before you act."

Celest sat a moment or two in thought and went back to see if she could open the door to continue. The door remained firmly shut, so she turned back, thinking that perhaps the key to the door was in the golden box. Celest placed each hand on a golden latch. Not knowing why, she felt her body grow tense as she opened it. Once the lid was opened, a fiery creature exploded out and sent streams of fire in Celest's direction. Celest pulled her cloak tightly around her and while it did keep her from getting burnt, she was still slammed against a nearby wall. She gasped as the air was knocked out of her body. The flaming beast howled wildly as it ripped its way around the room. As Celest stood up, she hugged her now-bruised ribs with her left arm. While with her right, she was just about to create a wind blade as she had done against the dark jackal in order to silence it. She was just about to let her own attack fly when she could not help but to hear its voice.

Celest lowered her right hand as she said to herself, "It's not an enemy…it's in pain." Celest pointed to the barrels of water and caused them to create a thick, wet fog which then turned into a soothing drizzle that would sooth the fiery beast. As the fire was put out, Celest could make out its true form. It was a small creature made of blue liquid crystal.

It smiled up at her and said, "Keep me with you until you are finished here. You who hold the flames of compassion in your heart." With that said it turned itself into a tiny crystal key. Slightly shaken, Celest made her way back to the red door. When she placed her hand on the knob she was surprised to find the door swung open freely. She was more surprised still, to see that the castle beyond the door had changed. Instead of opening up into the great corridor she had walked down earlier, there was a wooden stairwell leading downward. The old wood looked bluish gray in the light of the blue torches that lined it. As Celest got halfway down the stairwell, the sound of rushing water filled her ears.

When Celest had finally reached the bottom step she found herself facing what looked like a mighty river coursing towards her, and disappearing as it touched the wooden step beneath her feet. If this had been the real world she would have guessed that it was sometime in early spring.

As this thought occurred to her the voice from earlier filled the area, "A true warrior knows when it is appropriate to surrender. Do you have this knowledge?"

Celest's fist tightened at the very thought of giving up. Without further thought she stepped down and into the oncoming rush of water. The water was incredibly cold, and every now and then a chunk of ice would break free crashing into her body. She had no trouble believing that had it not been for her cloak she would have frozen to death. Gathering her thoughts she tried to cause the river to flow around her so that she could pass freely. But, the river seemed to have a will of its own and refused to cooperate. All that Celest was able to manage was to slow the river in front of her enough so, with great effort, she could slowly make headway.

After hours of work, Celest could see another stair well leading out of the icy river in the distance. Her body was numb with the cold, and her breath was labored with the task set before her. There were times when large chunks of ice bashed against her knocking her back several feet. But still she forced herself to continue on. It was when she had at last reached the step that her will power was tested further still.

As she stepped up onto it she found it covered with black ice. She slipped and fell back into the cold unforgiving river, which carried her a quarter mile back before she could stop herself. Celest cried with frustration, but only for a moment. Regaining her resolve she said to herself,

"If a warrior knows when to give up I'd rather be something else!" And with renewed determination she fought her way back to the steps leading out of the river. She was thinking of a way to get out of the water without slipping when the clear ice gathered itself together and showed its true form. It was another creature of liquid crystal, but this one was red.

It looked gently at Celest and down the river from where she had come before saying, "Keep me with you until your task here is done, you whose resolve is as cool as the arctic tundra. Celest climbed out of the river and onto the steps. The stairway that was now ahead of her was nearly identical to the last, only the torches were not blue. These torches held a scarlet flame that bathed her body with penetrating warmth. After fifty-two steps, Celest was pleased to find her clothing had completely dried out. Her only complaint was the exhaustion and pain that constantly pulled at her body. These problems were soon magnified further as she realized that the stairwell which she was climbing was at least three times as tall as the one going down. It was when Celest considered that she might be trapped in a time loop within the folded time in which she quested, that an immense sandstone door came into sight.

As Celest approached it she noticed two keyholes. At once the two keys spoke, "You have done well. We shall now open the path." They floated out from Celest's cloak and slid into their key holes like liquid gossamer. Celest was just about to open the door when the door and the keys faded away leaving an enormous archway. She paused for a moment to brace herself before boldly stepping into the room beyond.

The walls of the chamber were made of silver crystal. The ground was composed of gravel that was as black as midnight itself. Laying on top of the black gravel was a long carpet made of coarsely spun red silk. The carpet led to a small golden table at the end of the room. On the table rested the tool for which Celest had risked her life. The wall beyond the table consisted of a silver mirror lined in gold and platinum lace. As Celest approached the mirror her gaze was transfixed on her own reflection. With each step her image grew older, and her beauty also became more and more pronounced. Her dark hair grew in length, and as she grew taller her face took on the same elegance she loved about her mother's. Celest was nearly at the table when she noticed that the warmth had left her reflection's eyes. It pained her to see the eyes she had inherited from her mother void of the joy she had grown accustomed to having with her family. Desperate to get away in order to prevent such a fate from coming to pass she lunged for the tool. Before she could close her hand on the item that would end her quest in folded time, her older reflection stepped out of the mirror and gripped her already aching wrist with a grip that could make a river troll cry like a baby. Celest winced as the other spoke, "Do not be so hasty. We have our future to discuss. Once the Oblivion King has passed, what will you do? As the victor you could take up his powers. Our family would never be endangered again! Nothing would be beyond our powers! Look at me, I rule the world with an iron fist and life could not be better!"

Celest fought to free herself from the dark reflection's grasp, "I don't think so! You are not happy! You're not even human any more!"

The dark Celest's eyes narrowed as she sighed, "The hard way then." Black flame covered Celest's trapped wrist before her evil counterpart let go. Celest shrieked in pain as she held her burning wrist away from the rest of her body. She caused powerful gusts of wind, trying to blow out the dark flames that threatened to consume her. The black flames continued to hold on stubbornly. The dark reflection laughed out loud as Celest tried to smother the flame with the black gravel. Celest grew enraged at the other's jeering.

She pointed at it shouting, "You heartless monster!" A hundred pieces of gravel shot in the evil Celest's direction with the speed and power of bullets.

The Oblivion King's would-be replacement smiled cruelly as she waved the deadly projectiles away, "Have you forgotten I have all your powers? What is more, mine are boosted by unimaginable power, the power of darkness." Suddenly the dark version of Celest had kicked her to the ground and was standing on her still burning wrist, "Make it easy on us. Just accept the power. Swear it!" As her enemy shouted her last sentence, the pain in her body and burning wrist grew ten times worse. In fact it hurt her so badly that had she been anyone else she would have lost consciousness. But Celest had other things planned.

Focusing on what she had to say she replied, "There is no point in replacing the evil I am trying to stop!" Suddenly the pain stopped, and the evil older version of Celest froze on the spot. Beams of light escaped her body as cracks began to cover it. It was as if she were made of stained glass, and like glass she crumbled. Where the dark Celest once stood, an image of Celest's true future smiled with eyes full of warmth.

As she faded away she laughed, "Now we can honestly say that we have a good idea of who we are." Celest looked down at her wrist for signs of damage. While her body still ached, her wrist was completely fine.

Behind her the voice she had heard during her quest spoke once again, "Impressive, you have proven that I have not been waiting here in vain. But now, I need to rest. Keeping this space made was hard work, you know. And all that work has made me look like an old lady!" Celest turned to see a fairy. It was the only fairy Celest had seen touched by the ravages of time. She looked like an older, female version of Oscar. Celest knew that this must be his ancestor.

Celest looked sad as she asked, "Will you ever get to be young again?"

The elder fairy's smile crinkled the corners of her eyes, "Don't fret, I just need a little rest and I'll be good as new. Now take what is yours."

Celest watched as the little woman landed and with a flash of light became an enchanted rose. She smiled to herself as she turned to pick up the hard-earned item. It looked like an ivory sword handle. While it lacked a blade, it had different gems that ran up its sides in pairs. The first pair of gems, near the bottom of the handle, were deep scarlet. When she looked closer at them, Celest could see a raging inferno blazing in their depths. The next pair up the handle was pale blue, and these seemed to be like tiny windows overlooking the sea. Inside she could see waves stirring within the gems' surfaces. Next, the handle had gems that were amber colored. When Celest looked closely at these, she saw earthquakes shaking the foundations of the world around them. The pair of gems at the top were pale gray, as she gazed into their depths she saw miniature tornados idly spinning on the spot. The place a blade would have normally protruded from, a deep bluish gray stone was set deep into the handle. Inside flashes of lighting could be seen, powerful gusts of wind tore at the clouds around them. Celest tucked the tool into her back pocket, and took out Oscar's crown. Tightly closing her eyes she thought of her brothers and close friends. When she opened them again she was nuzzled to the ground by an expectant Stormy. He looked her over as if trying to see if she came back with all the body parts she left with. Celest hugged Stormy and her brothers who had just gotten around Stormy to see her. She apologized for making them worry, before returning Oscar his crown and hugging Terra. Oscar smiled and said, "That tool will help you greatly. You truly deserve it."

Celest looked over at him saying, "This whole time we have referred to it as a tool, but what is its name?"

Oscar laughed, "What would you name it? It only focuses your own abilities."

She shrugged, "How about the elemental heart? It seems to be full of the elements that are at the heart of my power."

Oscar's face grew a little more serious, "A fine name. But listen to me when I say that your true power comes not from the elements but from *your* essence, and the love you share with your cherished ones."

Terra was looking at the elemental heart closely, "Elemental stones, but those are so rare that they are said to only exist in fables. Could you show them to us in action?"

Celest smiled, "It would be an honor!" As she brought

the gift to her side a long fiery whip extended from its tip. Celest snapped it in the air a few times spelling *thank you for believing in me* in midair with flaming letters. Moments after she had caused the whip to retract into the handle, a large razor sharp ice saber emerged. Her cloak billowed out as she leaped high into the air and, using her frozen blade, erased the words. Once she landed, the ice saber melted, and in its place a large stone hammer emerged. She struck the ground in front of her with it and sent a shock wave rippling in front of her. She held up her left hand, the one not holding the elemental heart, and caused large rocks to soar in her direction. She did not try to change their course. Nor did she try to dodge them; instead she held the now hammerless handle in front of her and the rocks shattered against an invisible shield of wind. Oscar applauded and Terra smiled approvingly.

After a while John flew over and landed on his sister's shoulder and said, "Wow...but you look so tired. What did you have to do to get it?" Celest gave him a swift explanation of her time in folded time.

John looked exceedingly proud of his sister as he said, "Cool, now you don't have to be so creative with your environment. It's like a shortcut to the elements you want to use. No more making fire from rocks—unless you want to, that is."

After a couple minutes Oscar said, "Right, well Iron Back lives on Mt. Krono. It is just a two-day flight from here. Celest you should rest on the way, and I would like you to drink six cups of lightning leaf tea between here and there. With that said, off we go!"

Iron Back and

the Golden Turtle

The Windhearts, now being used to long journeys, felt like they had just left Bulaklak Haven when they arrived at Mt. Krono. It was easily the tallest mountain in the range. Its peak was crowned with a halo of white fluffy clouds. Stormy seemed to know where he was going as he landed right in front of the mouth of a large cave. Terra took the lead as they ventured into the cave. The air itself seemed to rumble with the breathing sound of a large and ancient creature. As they entered the innermost chamber, they noticed the immense form that filled the corner of the cave. As they approached, a large rust colored eye snapped open.

Oscar's right hand flew instinctively to his sword but as he began to draw it a deep rumbling voice filled the chamber, "Still your sword, pixie. I have not eaten the flesh of a sentient creature for two millennia past. Though, it has been months since I have eaten at all. Not since…" The dragon's voice faded into silence.

Celest stepped closer and asked gently, "Not since when, Mr. Iron Back?" noticing for the first time how his gray scaly hide clung tightly to his bones. His lips pulled into what, Celest was sure, was meant to be a smile.

Iron Back looked with admiration at her concern, "Not since the Oblivion King killed my mate. You see, she had gone off to find us some cattle or something that we would have found acceptable to eat. At some point during her trip the Oblivion King approached her and wanted her to join his ranks. He told her that the cold one had already joined up, and that he was having his fill of delicious elves and other such creatures to feed on. She and I had been together for longer than I can remember, and that is quite a long time. I can still remember when this mountain was just a fault line where earthquakes happened regularly. That was some twenty-five millennia past. At any rate, this revolted her rather than tempted her. She refused him and he killed her on the spot. I heard that you gave the ice dragon the beating of his life. Well done!"

Oscar cut in, "Your sources of information are faulty. They killed him!"

Iron Back eyed him coolly and said, "Don't be so quick to consider me wrong. As you well know, I was already ancient when your people were still new. In fact, the only one as old as me standing in this chamber is that storm steed over there…pleasure to finally make your acquaintance." Stormy bowed his head causing his long main to partially cover his face. "Unless I am much mistaken, which could happen to anyone, but in this case unlikely, the ice dragon's essence could have merely been scattered to the four winds. He could be brought back to his true form should his essence ever be reunited. It could take a month, a year, fifty years, or perhaps never. It infuriates me that that sorry excuse for a dragon, that filthy serpent, has that type of immortality while my mate." Iron back broke off yet again.

It was Celest who broke the silence yet again, "Sir, we have come seeking the rings of Aquados. We are determined to bring the Oblivion King down. Will you please help us?"

He looked at her as if he had just noticed her presence for the first time, "Yes, of course." He leaned down and placed five platinum rings on the ground before Celest and said, "The quickest path to the sea lies beneath the lake near Bulaklak Haven. And to use it you will need this."

Two thin streams of fire shot from Iron Back's nostrils and where they hit the ground a golden key shimmered in the half light of the cave. As Celest picked it up she noticed the key's handle was carved in the image of a merman locked in fierce battle with a shark that had sprouted muscular legs and arms. Each was holding a harpoon. Iron Back was just about to speak again when he looked up in alarm. His ears seemed to be keener than other creatures. He opened his mouth wide and a blast of fire issued out filling the entrance to the cave.

As he smashed the rear wall of the cave with his tail he whispered urgently, "There is normally a secret door there that could be opened with a long series of passwords. However we had not the time, have the elemental wielder seal it shut again. Now go, there is not much time."

Once everyone was safely on the other side of the

doorway, Iron Back watched mutely as Celest sealed it shut. Quietly he turned to face the flaming entrance. After a few tense moments a creature wearing black leather came strolling through the flames. It looked like a human garbed in ninja gear, and could have been had it not been for the pitch dark mist that poured freely from his reptilian eyes.

Iron Back sneered with amusement as he spoke, "So, you think you can take the heat do you?" Quicker than a jaguar he snatched the creature up and held it directly in front of his mouth. An instant later his mouth opened and an enormous blast of fire engulfed the creature and Iron Back's hand. Once the flame had dissipated, only the remaining ashes of the humanoid monster drifted silently to the ground, Iron Back's clawed hand now closed on empty air.

Five minutes passed in silence, but Iron Back knew that this encounter was far from over. Suddenly eight more of the strange creatures emerged from the wall of fire, all drawing cruelly hewn swords. Next, the same dark knight that had assaulted John emerged from the flame.

Iron Back looked at him appraisingly, "You seem more powerful than the rest, no matter, I will prevent you from harming those children." Iron Back reared onto his hind legs and then slammed himself back down, digging his clawed fingers deep into the stone ground and spreading his great leathery wings. The air around him became distorted with heat waves as his gray metallic scales began to glow as they turned from gray, to blue, to red, to white hot. With out further warning he opened his mouth wide and a long, intense pillar of fire exploded from the depths of his throat. The inferno filled the entire cave with flame.

When the fire cleared, Iron Back stood five feet behind where he had started. Deep claw marks could be seen in the cave's floor where the force of his attack had pushed him back despite his firm hold on it. He looked forward in an enraged silence. All of the small creatures were gone. The knight, however, had managed to block his onslaught. The black knight drew his twelve foot sword and walked directly toward the dragon. His blade was poised to strike.

The Windhearts stopped walking as a loud roar shook the path down which they were escaping. The complete silence that followed was what truly unnerved them. Celest turned to Terra and said, "I am going back! He needs help. What if he is hurt?"

Terra shook her head, "If *that* dragon was hurt, then there is nothing you can do for him now. You still have much room for improvement. If he has indeed been killed, he died trying to buy you and your brothers time to get stronger. Do not let his death be in vain. I think he wants you to avenge his mate, and possibly himself." Celest reluctantly followed as they once again headed down the winding path.

As they emerged from the cave, cool moonlight played gently across their faces. Celest reflected bitterly as they walked. She thought about how since their arrival in this world they made many friends. And all these friends were ready to lay their lives on the line to keep them from harm. Unfortunately, she also knew that no matter how many friends they made, in the end it would all come down to her and her brothers versus the Oblivion King. Celest wondered how her mom was doing. They had been away so long, and their mother was all alone. Celest felt her eyes begin to sting and then she felt a warm hand on her shoulder.

Terra's voice came from behind her, "Iron Back is fine…at least I am pretty sure of it. You want to talk…any questions perhaps?" Celest slowly turned around to see Terra wearing a warm smile.

After a minute or two Celest said, "I was just thinking about what we have to do, about Iron Back, and about… my mom. But, you know, I do have a question. How did Iron Back know that I could wield elements?"

Terra's answer came so quickly that Celest was sure that, in this world at least, the answer was common knowledge, "In this world, the dragon's eye sight is second only to the golden eagle. Iron Back must have 'looked' into you and saw some of your abilities."

After about three miles of walking, Oscar told everyone that it was probably safe to fly. The reason they walked so far instead of just flying, was that if they were to just fly right away, they'd more likely be followed. Once airborne, the journey to Bulaklak Haven went relatively fast. Their stay in Oscar's kingdom was very short. A few hours after Oscar had updated Marlene on the situation, and had given her instructions on things he wanted done for his kingdom, they left for the lake that Stormy had brought Celest to see.

It was just as vast as Celest remembered it. If anything, it seemed larger; no doubt due to the fact that they were about to spend a lot of time under the water's surface. Oscar instructed everyone to put on their rings as he passed them out. Celest helped Eric and John put theirs on.

As she put Eric's ring on she noticed something that

she felt she should have noticed earlier, "We did not get enough rings. What about Stormy?"

Oscar smiled, "Oh him, well he does not need one. The main things making him up are wind and water, so he will be quite at home underneath the waves. Shall we?"

He turned and began to walk toward the lake's edge. Celest and her brothers went next closely followed by Terra and Stormy. The water was lukewarm and shimmered silently in the starlight. As Celest walked into the lake she could feel the water climbing up her body with every step, and as it reached her chin she began to panic. Even as she gasped for air she strode onward closing her eyes, acutely aware of the water that was now enveloping her. Suddenly, she felt as if she were still breathing in the night air.

When she opened her eyes she was several feet under the water's surface, the stars above them swaying happily to and fro with the lakes shifting surface. The runes on the rings Iron Back had given them blazed with an ice blue light. Celest turned to see how Stormy was doing. He looked the same as always, the clouds making up his body were still swirling relentlessly, only now they seemed to be full of millions of tiny air bubbles.

She then turned to John and said, "This is weird, but kind of cool, huh?"

John laughed nervously, "Yeah, but I wonder how we can talk to each other under here." John looked around indicating that he was still talking about the lake.

Celest shrugged, "Probably because of these rings, I guess. I wonder if we will eat inside our bags. I really don't want to be swallowing this water. Fish use it as a bathroom, you know. Hey, because of you, the penguin is not the only bird that can live under the water!"

John laughed hollowly, "Great, now the things down here that normally eat penguins can try something new. Eagles—the other bird meat."

Eric, on the other hand, seemed to be perfectly comfortable under the water. Maybe this is because children under two do not understand that they do not belong under water like this. They walked deeper and deeper into the lake. From above them an unearthly sound flooded the world around them. The moment it reached their ears, the center pieces of the charms Oscar had given John and Eric began to glow with a soft golden light. Celest found the noise very annoying. John and Eric seemed to like it well enough, but John admitted that it got very old after a while.

Terra walked beside Celest as she said, "Sirens, women can't stand the sound of their hideous voices, but men can't resist their call."

Celest laughed as Terra answered her unasked question, "Thanks, so that's why the ring that Oscar gave me, when I first visited his kingdom, is not glowing like John's and Eric's gifts. My ring does not need to protect my mind. Girls are immune."

Terra nodded and added, "If you'll notice, Oscar's crown is glowing with the same light your brother's charms are. Not even male fairies can resist without help. The only male I have ever seen ignore their power is trotting ahead of us. Stormy is the type of creature that will never easily bend to the will of others."

The little group of adventurers traveled for so long that the Windhearts felt as if they would never reach their destination. Just when John was about to ask how long it would take them to get where they were going, they reached a large rock formation that looked like an abnormally large sea turtle. Its shell was caked so thickly with marine vegetation and grime, it appeared to have been under the lake's surface for at least a century or more.

After studying the formation for a moment Oscar turned to Celest, "If you would please clean this thing up for us. As always, it would be appreciated."

She nodded and held up her left hand. The water around the rock statue began to spin and started to pick up sand as it went. After a few moments the statue could not be seen at all. Only a cloudy torrent of earth could be seen, and the difference it made was immediately recognizable once it had settled. The turtle's shell turned out to be made of gold with fire opals and pearls embedded in its hard surface.

Oscar gestured for the others to follow him and said, "The rings of Aquados automatically let you move under water in the same way you would on land. But if you ever want to swim, just go for it. The rings will sense your desire and allow you to do so, don't worry, even when you are swimming you will still be able to breathe. Come on." He flew to the top of the turtle's shell and the others swam after him, except for John and Stormy, of course, who also flew.

Once on the turtle's back, Celest found Oscar kneeling over a strange carving on its surface. It was a carving portraying the same symbol on the key that Iron Back had given them. Before Oscar had asked her to do so, she had already taken the key out of her back pocket and handed it to him. Oscar thanked her and placed the key into the hole that was directly between the shark beast and the merman. The side of the shell to the right of the turtle's head slid cleanly to the ground revealing a set of stairs that led into a pitch black tunnel. Oscar went in first. The moment he stepped onto the first step, tiny worms on the walls lit the tunnel with an eerie turquoise light. They walked along the twisting tunnel for twelve hours, only stopping twice to rest. At last the tunnel opened up, and beyond the opening the ocean greeted them. And a mere mile ahead of them, an underwater kingdom awaited them.

Mrs. Windheart

Perhaps it is time we went back into the world the Windhearts came from for a moment…our world. Mrs. Windheart was having a very hard and tiring day. Her missing children weighed on her mind like an overgrown elephant seeking a piggyback ride. She had called in at work telling them that, "I need to find my kids! I just can't come in today. Any wasted time is time that something horrible could be happening to them." She spent all day at the police station pacing; during this time her frustration only grew. She had spent the past few days in the same manner. A large cop with a pug-like face was asking questions, and making statements that Mrs. Windheart felt were a complete waste of time.

He drank from his mug and then said, "Are you sure they're missing and not just at a friend's house or something?"

Mrs. Windheart replied in a flustered voice, "My kids have been gone for days on end. They have not called to ask my permission to stay somewhere else. If they wanted to stay at a friend's or something they would have asked! It is how I brought them up. Here is something else for you to think about! How would my oldest son go to *a friend's house* when last I knew, his school called me and said that he was in a hospital room? My youngest is not even two years old! So I doubt he would be going anywhere on his own! "

The cop took another sip from his mug and asked, "Where's their father? You would think that he would be concerned about their absence." Mrs. Windheart stopped pacing for a moment and sat down.

Shaking her head she replied, "He…lives out of town."

The cop did not seem to notice, or care, that this could be a touchy subject as he continued. "So you two are separated? Is there a chance that he *took* the children?"

Mrs. Windheart flared up at once saying, "While it is true that we are *separated*, I doubt that he would take them without notifying me!"

The policeman looked very much unabashed as he said, "If you want to see your kids again we must consider all suspects. We will get someone on the case as soon as possible." Mrs. Windheart stood up and put her hands on the cop's desk.

Leaning forward she looked the cop in the eyes as she snarled, "What? You mean to tell me that you are going to put the safety of my children on the back burner? What could possibly be more important?"

The cop took another sip from his coffee mug and closed the file he had on the table as he said, "Mrs. Windheart, you are not the only parent that we are trying to locate their children for. We have a very limited workforce, but as I said, we will get someone on the case as soon as possible."

By the time Mrs. Windheart got home it had began to rain so hard that even with her windshield wipers going at full speed she could barely see the road. Once she got there she dragged herself to her room and grabbed a towel on the way. As she sat on her bed and dried her hair she stared at the rain hammering against the window. She sat there for a moment in a kind of trance and quietly said, "I wonder."

Inner Strength

Now, back to the world which the Windhearts later only referred to as "that other place." As they walked toward the kingdom, Celest's hair softly drifted out behind her on watery currents. While she did not know exactly why, she felt as if something was disastrously wrong. Her worst fears were confirmed as they entered the grand city's gates. They were surrounded by mer-people. While it was easy to tell that they were naturally a beautiful people, they were not remotely as beautiful as they could be now. Their color seemed to have been drained from their bodies. They were all in a gray monochrome, like an old black and white T.V. show. They barely showed any signs of being alive. They did not move on their own, but drifted sadly back and forth with the shifting ocean tides.

As John asked, "What happened here?" a little squid swam up and was acting quite strangely. In fact it was acting more like a dog that wanted its owner to follow it than it was acting like a squid.

Terra offered, "I think it wants to take us somewhere, maybe we should follow?" Oscar and Stormy nodded, moments later they were following a strange little creature through a kingdom they never knew. It led them directly to the castle's gates. The tiny squid then slid between the bars and pinched itself into the little gap where the giant door, behind the gates, met the paved ground. Seconds later the gates, and the enormous door clanked open. Once they had entered the castle a large group of the king's servants greeted them. Among these servants was a guard of eight warriors. These mer-people looked nothing like the poor souls who drifted around aimlessly outside. No, these were mer-people as they should be, full of both color and life. Two of the tallest guards swam forward in greeting. One had skin as pale as moon dust and a dark blue tail streaked with rainbows. The other looked as if his top half was chiseled out of black marble and his tail called to mind a sunrise with all its shades of red, orange, and yellow.

The two smiled brightly and said in unison, "Our king is pleased to have guests from the world above once again. Please, come and see him at once."

Oscar smiled in return and said, "Well, it would be rude to keep him waiting, lead the way." The mermen turned and swam ahead closely followed by Eric. It seems that he found their colorful tails enticing. Upon entering they found the king watching his pet squid with great amusement. The squid was still acting like a mutated puppy. If it had a tail it would undoubtedly be chasing it. As it was, however, he looked as if he were trying to catch his long tentacles. When the king turned to face his guests, Celest noticed that he looked just like the "ruler of the sea" she had read about in storybooks at school. His tail was long and powerful and was bluish-green. His top half was as well muscled as his bottom half. His sharp blue eyes made his golden crown look very plain. In his hand was not a royal scepter but a grand platinum trident.

His long white beard and mustache floated out in front of him as he smiled and said, "Welcome, please sit down. If you could please tell me how you came to be here and why. I hate to seem rude, but these are not the best times and we have not had surface dwellers here for at least two hundred years." Oscar immediately told the king their story up until their arrival in his kingdom. When he had finished the king scratched his chin thoughtfully and said, "Yes, I have heard of this Oblivion King. His deadly grasp has recently reached us here on the ocean floor. You no doubt have noticed his 'messengers' work on your way to my castle, my poor people. Now, while I am thankful for help, it is not our way to endanger children." Celest realized that the king must have brought the children of the entire kingdom into his castle. She didn't see any on the way there.

She could not help but wonder, "Your majesty, what happened to their parents…the children, I mean."

The king's sharp blue gaze fell on Celest and softened as he said, "My sweet child, they were attacked by a dark creature I feel may have once been a siren. Normally their powers only work on males but this one is different. Have you never wondered what happened to one once his mind was under the control of a siren? Even after their vessel was smashed upon jagged rocks? They are drained. This is the true reason sirens have for doing this to people—its how they eat. Their victims are robbed of their will to live, and robbed of that which makes them, well, them. I am telling you that sirens feed on their victim's personalities. The Windhearts looked thunderstruck at hearing this and fell into silence.

The mer-king continued, "That is why my people are floating around out there helpless. They sent their children to me and tried to fight off the evil beast themselves. Normally I can protect the entire kingdom of Heaven's Mirror with my trident…but we face too powerful a foe. I will not allow you to share our fate! As I can at least protect my castle, you can rest here before your return journey in relative safety."

Celest sat in thought for a moment and said, "You know, I think we will share your fate." Before the king could interrupt she continued, "My brothers, my friends, and I am not as powerless as you would think we are. The reason I say that we will share your fate is because we would like to. We would like to, because we are going to make sure it is a happy one, your highness."

The king looked like he was going to object for a moment but said, "If you're that determined then I will not stand in your way. But as you are helping to protect my people, calling me things like 'your majesty' and 'your highness' will not do. Please call me Ladagat."

Celest who never cared for beating around the bush said, "Thank you, Ladagat. I would like to go after this monster right away. Which way did she come from last?"

The king looked impressed at her go-get-them attitude but said, "Please don't be so foolhardy my child. Even the best of us need to sleep. It's not that I doubt your abilities, of course not; you have defeated many powerful foes already. This monster has a 'friend' that helps it attack.

Its friend is a powerful ocean snake. It causes tremendous water surges, and its venom is why my people out there have lost their color. So rest for the intense battle ahead, and enjoy my home for a while."

Celest and her party did the only sensible thing they could and took King Ladagat's advice. It turned out that they were going to eat and sleep inside the largest bag. That night they had a meal consisting of pork chops, mashed potatoes and gravy, and many healthy portions of corn on the cob drenched with butter. To drink was cool zana, which to Celest tasted like orange flavored soda at the time. As she lay in the bag's cool and pleasantly dry interior, waves of sleep blew over her and carried her to her own warm room.

Celest walked over to her bed and sat beside her younger self and said, "I really hope that monster comes. I am sure that it is the Oblivion King and I've got a thing or two I want to tell that monster!"

The little girl smiled and said, "I don't think he will be coming. Look out the window." Celest got up and looked outside. The rose bushes that once lined the fence had all grown twenty feet high. As they grew, their branches all meshed together so tightly that a grasshopper would have had trouble getting through. The roses were as diverse as regular roses could be, but instead of red, white, pink, yellow and all the different patterns they came in, these were roses made up of the elements that Celest now knew she could call upon to aid her. A few of these flowers were flaming smoldering fire roses, solid granite roses, flowing shining watery roses, and wispy cloudy roses. All of which were spinning like tiny windmills and moved the night air silently among themselves.

From behind her she heard her younger self say, "You are now strong enough to keep that monster out of your head. While you no longer need to *see* me, don't forget me. And never forget where you came from once you consciously know." When Celest turned to face her she saw her younger self fading into thin air, and she found herself waking up. She felt sad and happy and slightly confused at the same time, a strange feeling indeed.

Celest looked around and saw that everyone was still asleep. She looked over at Eric and saw that he was once again holding a pillow above his head with his feet. Smiling to herself she tiptoed to the backpack's entrance and pushed open the flap. Her ring of Aquados blazed into life the moment she was submerged once again. To her surprise, a group of mer-children were waiting for her and barraged her with questions about the world beyond their waters. Celest was just in the process of telling the children what wind was when she heard Terra's voice saying, "Morning! Did you sleep alright?" Celest turned to see everyone coming up out of the bag followed by an air bubble filled Stormy.

She smiled brightly and replied, "I slept great! How are you guys?"

Oscar was the one who answered, "Good, but hungry. Let's go back into the bag and have some breakfast. Then we have to meet King Ladagat at eleven for a tour of his castle. He told me so last night."

Before they could go into the bag to eat, a young mer-boy with a tail that was the sort of yellow you'd see in the fall, darted into the room and said, "You will let me help you when it is time to face *her*. She has got to pay for what she did to my parents! I can help. I am real strong."

Celest turned to face him and felt sorry for the boy. He was about the same age as John. She walked up to him and put her hand on his shoulder, "I am sure you're real tough. But I already have my friends and brothers helping me. Don't worry, we will give them one and make sure they know that it is from you."

His little face twisted with a mixture of despair and frustration. He jerked himself out of her hand and tore out of the room. Celest stood there for a moment after she watched his tail disappear around the corner. Slowly she turned to go with the others to eat. When they had finished with breakfast, which was oats for Stormy and cheesy eggs with toast for everyone else, they met with Ladagat in his throne room. He led them down a long corridor which ended with a revolving door that seemed to be carved out of smoky quartz. About halfway down Celest told him about the little boy. Ladagat nodded gravely, "That must be Kevano. His parents were the first to suffer. It was a terrible trip for him. They were the first to see the cretins coming. They rushed him to my castle gates. The evil beasts caught his father first…then his mother. He soon found himself fleeing for his life all alone. He was the one who alerted me to the dark presence. I fear that the loss of his parents has made him bitter."

Celest thought how losing her mom would make her feel and then asked, "Will they get better once we put a stop to the monsters?"

As they reached the door Ladagat shrugged, "Only God can tell. Well now, I think you may find this interesting."

Once they had gone through, they found themselves in a bluish-gray room. The half of the room that they had entered in from was filled with water. The other was as dry as a desert wind. Shortly after they had entered, a woman that reminded Celest of one of the heroines from one of her favorite stories entered the room from behind her, followed by six of the kids she met earlier. Just to give you an idea of what the woman looked like, the character that Celest liked was the proud daughter of a great sultan. As we are talking about a mermaid I will also tell you that her tail was a deep scarlet.

She turned to the children and said, "You are to wait here and watch. I am going to show you all basic walking and running. And I will also show you what you will learn if you should attend the advance classes, mainly, star-runner techniques." Without another word she sped toward the dry side of the room while swimming near the ceiling. She exploded out of the water and Eric closed his eyes. He never liked to watch other people getting hurt, and it looked like she was going to get a face full of the stone floor. Celest's eyes filled with wonder.

The woman's tail flashed neon green for a moment and then was replaced with a pair of legs. She tumbled through the air and gracefully landed. She was now wearing a pair of flowing baggy silk pants that were the same shade of scarlet that her tail was.

She smiled at her student's amazement, "Are you surprised that Ms. Serena can be so agile? Well, you have not seen anything yet." She then began to walk slowly so that the kids could see exactly what she was doing. She brought up the pace to a speed walk. Then up again to a jog. Next she began to sprint around the room. She laughed wildly as she yelled to her students, "Are you ready for the main event?" Purple and green sparks seemed to appear out of thin air and were sucked by an invisible force into the soles of her feet. With a burst of speed she ran straight up a wall. Once she reached the top she kicked off of it and was running along another wall horizontally toward her students. She slammed through the wall of water and a flash of neon purple light dispersed to reveal her powerful tail. Still grinning she told her students, "If you were unaware, that last portion was a star-runner technique. It comes easy to us because when our tails change into legs none of our muscle structure is lost. It is wise for you to continue with your D.L.C. That is, your Dry Land Classes. You are as much a part of the land as you are of the sea, dismissed."

TRANSFORMATION OF
LOVE AND LOYALTY

As the students left the room Celest turned to Terra and Oscar, "This is amazing! This is like a world of fairytales come to life. In our world mermaids get legs when they come on land too!"

Terra laughed, "It is true that in legends and myths there is often a strand of truth woven in among the things...made up. If you like those kinds of stories, then you will soon agree that it is the true stories that are the most interesting."

John looked at Terra and said, "But don't true stories become myths and legends? It is natural for things to fall apart and then be forgotten. That strand of truth you were talking about is just a piece of a broken true story, right?"

Terra looked impressed at the thought John put behind his words. After a moment she said, "True, but the true stories worth remembering will last forever. One day the story about the Windhearts will be well worth telling. Now, all this talk of stories, reminds me. Would you guys like to here a tale of unyielding courage and loyalty?"

King Ladagat's face seemed to light up as he said, "Please, I would love to here an elfin tale."

Terra took a moment to gather her thoughts and began, "Once, long ago, when I was around Celest's age, my father told me this story. There was once a young boy. As his name is a secret for now. Let's call him Smith. Smith and his family had left their land to escape a horrible fate. Now what that fate was is a story for another time. On their journeys, looking for a new land to call their home, Smith only had his brother to talk to. His brother was named Atlantio. But as he was barely talking and Smith was ten; their conversations were very basic. Smith loved his family beyond words. In spite of the woes they had to endure they remained close to one another. If anything, the pain they had to endure only strengthened their love for each other. One day, shortly after crossing a great canyon, a horrible group of cut-throat bandits dragged their wagon in front of their path. The leader of the bandits said, 'Give me your prized possessions and I may not kill your cute little children there.'

"The dad did the only sensible thing a man who cared for his family's safety could do. He walked up to the crook and took off his diamond encrusted armlet and gave it to the man. 'Now leave us in peace,' he said as he shoved his arm guard into the bandit's hands.

"The man laughed, 'Now why would I do that? Such a lovely wife you have.'

"As he made toward Smith's mom, his dad stepped between them. Swift as a thunderbolt the lead bandit was laying on his face with his own dagger stuck in his left leg. Smith's dad looked at the large group of remaining bandits and said, 'Please, leave us in peace. And collect your boss.'

"One of the bandits climbed on top of the wagon and began throwing bottles at them. When the bottles broke on the ground a green haze floated up from them and Smith and his family knew only darkness. When everyone came to, Smith found himself being roughly held by his shoulders. The first thing he saw was his family dangling by a thin thread of light. The bandits had put them in a cage hanging off the side of the canyon they had just crossed. One of the bandits hobbled forward. I say that he hobbled forward because he had a wooden leg. Once he was in front of Smith he said, 'Your pops over there did me boss a great dishonor, boy. But, we ain't unkind, eh? What we will do is let you hold your family up until someone comes to your aid, easy eh?'

"At these words three men with thick leather gloves pulled toward Smith the thread of light he knew was holding his family above the canyon. Upon a closer look, the light turned out to be a very thin but very strong wire. The bandit who was talking earlier said, 'Now then…you gonna help your family boy?'

"Smith's dad shouted from his suspended prison, 'Don't do it. We will fall no matter what you do. There is no sense in you getting hurt in the process.'

"Smith looked at his dad as a bandit threw an empty bottle against the cage, the broken glass showering against his trapped family. He sobbed slightly and he nodded. The bandit with a wooden leg laughed, 'That a boy. You be real brave for such a kid. I grant ya one request.'

"Smith looked the bandit dead into his eyes, 'Wrap that wire three times around my hand. I don't want to slip.'

"The crowd of bandits roared with laughter. Even among the uproar Smith could hear his mother weeping with despair. Smith held out his right hand and the bandits seized it. Even as they were looping the sharp wire around his palm it cut into him, his blood began to drip. Once the bandits let go the wire began to drag Smith across the ground. He cried out as he held on with every fiber of his being. He could hear his dad telling him to let go, and his mother yelling the same. He could also hear his little brother crying. As he slid over the rough ground he managed to get his left hand around a large rock and he held fast. The blood poured more freely from his right and the pain intensified.

"He wished from every corner of his soul that he had the power to save his family. He held on for so long that the bandits lost interest and left. Now, some say that God heard his heart's deepest wish. Others say that he wanted to save his family so badly that he simply willed it to happen. But suddenly he felt stronger. The mind-numbing pain he felt faded. He could feel his entire body getting taller, and growing firmer. His feet seemed to be digging into the earth growing thick and long. His hair seemed to shiver as the evening's breeze passed through it. His arms felt very stiff, but strong as a great oak. The blood on his right hand had disappeared. It turned into dry dead bark and fell to the earth which was now surprisingly far away. Smith had become a majestic and one of a kind tree. One of his branches reached into the cage that now held his family. It was as if he longed to touch them. Days passed, but his family did not go thirsty or starve. Smith now knew how to take the water and goodness from the earth to produce a lush snow white fruit. As they waited, Smith's family could hear the wind blowing though his leaves. And when this happened they could also hear him whispering words of encouragement, 'Don't give up. Be strong. Help will come soon.'

"Well as it happened, help did come. Smith's aunty on his mother's side eventually led a search party and rescued them. They could not stand to leave the tree that was once their son, so Smith's family decided to call that land home and made their village near there."

King Ladagat looked so sad that had he not already been under water, his eyes would have undoubtedly been full of tears. Celest shook her head and said, "What a sad story. But, why not tell us Smith's real name?"

Terra smiled, "Because *Smith* is my uncle and I would like you to ask him yourself. It will help you to see the truth of my words. The village is now called Rose Brew. Atlantio is my dad. I swear your story will one day be an undying legend."

Celest smiled and thanked Terra for her kind words and the story. Ladagat also thanked Terra and added to the children, "I will personally make a record about the way you helped my kingdom. Then I will make a decree causing it to become a royal treasure. It will remain unaltered as long as my people exist."

John's wings stretched out, and then flapped with excitement, "But for you to do that we've got to help you first. And we can't do that till we get out there and find…"

BATTLE BENEATH THE WAVES

John never got to finish his sentence. The room shook violently and pieces of the ceiling crumbled and fell to the floor. Five minutes later a girl with glasses and a tail that seemed to be patterned after a peacock's came flying through the revolving door. Her chest was heaving as she fought to catch her breath, "Your...high...ness...we...we...are...un...under...attack!"

King Ladagat's grip on his trident tightened as he looked at the Windhearts and said, "I am sorry. I cannot go with you out to face those fiends. I must stay here and fortify the castle. I cannot risk harm coming to the children. Please be safe."

With that said he held up his trident and then brought its tip down to touch the floor. The water felt thicker somehow, and then it left its usual lukewarm temperature and grew hot before becoming cooler than it normally was. It was like someone had pressed the rewind button on a home movie. The bits of the ceiling that had crumbled to the ground now tumbled back to the ceiling. Before their eyes the room began to repair itself. Then everything about the castle was becoming transparent, clear as crystal. Before they knew what was going on, they all felt as if they were just floating in the middle of the ocean. Other than the king, the castle and all its occupants had become invisible to everyone but John.

King Ladagat looked at the children with concern in his eyes, "In this state the castle is all but indestructible, and for the most part unseen. Again I need to apologize for not coming with you. Once my trident and I leave the castle it will return to normal. I will, however, save you the trouble of trying to find your way out of an invisible fortress, when you are ready."

Celest gave the old king a reassuring smile and nodded. With a wave of his trident, King Ladagat sent them on their way. Celest felt as if they were on dry land again caught in a high wind being blown around helplessly. Eric at least was enjoying the trip. Celest and John could hear his laughter behind them. As soon as they had grown used to the sensation, it was over and they were all outside the castle. In the distance they could see a small figure approaching them. Their breath caught slightly on the way in as the dark siren's image became clearer. This was the most frightening monster they had yet faced. What made her so scary was the fact that she simply resembled a beautiful woman. It was the air of deception that amplified the sense of danger, much like a magnifying glass focuses the sunlight into a blazing beam of destruction.

Once the siren was close enough to see her face clearly they could see the evil in her eyes. Her face was half hidden by a wispy veil of translucent green seaweed. The siren laughed lightly and said, "Ah, it appears that the good king is now sending us the appropriate tributes. Look at the meal he has sent to us."

Before John could ask Celest who the siren was talking to, a cloud of sand puffed up off the ocean floor. Once it had settled an ocean snake was eyeing them all hungrily. He was roughly the size of eight full grown anacondas, and his scales were cobalt. His eyes were red as fire ants, and he had a great hood like a cobra's. It sent a powerful current of water that knocked everyone to the floor and Stormy slightly off balance. Its mouth opened wide exposing its cruel fangs. Just as it was about to rush them, Stormy regained himself and tackled the evil sea serpent. Upon the collision, both the snake and the storm steed shot straight up to the ocean's surface. Even as they went, the azure serpent tried to throw his powerful coils around Stormy.

Everyone including the dark siren watched in awe as the two powerful creatures took their battle to another level. As they disappeared from sight, the malevolent enchantress turned her attention to her intended pray. She looked upon the remaining members of the Windhearts' party as a cold smile played at the corners of her full, red lips. The siren's mouth opened and her voice flowed out. It was enchanting, haunting, and nearly irresistible, "Relax, be joyous, and give yourselves to me."

The instant her first word left her mouth the charms Oscar had given to Celest, John, and Eric began to emit their soft golden light. Oscar's crown did likewise. Celest made a rude hand gesture and said, "I don't think so."

The siren's smile faltered and she cocked her head to the side and said to Celest, "There was a time when your defiance would not have surprised me. But, now I am no where near the weak creature I used to be. The Oblivion King has granted me true power. I am interested in those lovely trinkets you are wearing."

Before anyone could say or do anything, Kevano had found his way out of the castle and rushed the siren with a long dagger. The siren giggled wickedly and slapped the blade out of his hands. Then she snatched Kevano up by his hair and said to Celest, "How about you take off that pretty little ring of yours?"

The siren then placed her index finger nail against Kevano's throat. Her nails were all at least two inches long and razor sharp. Celest did not know what else to do. She took off her ring. The siren laughed, "Good, now restrain your allies." Celest felt as if she were watching herself in third person. She watched in horror as her own body turned, waved its right hand, and caused the earth they were all standing on to rise up and encase her brothers, Terra, and Oscar in a way that only allowed their heads to be exposed. The dark siren smiled wickedly and said, *"Now, kill them!"*

Celest felt a pounding inside her head. It was as if the siren's words were bouncing around the inside of her skull. Then it was as if a raging storm filled her head, and her own voice drifted to her on the fresh peals of thunder, "No, I will not. They are my family!" While Celest fought with herself, Eric who trusted his sister with his life simply went to sleep.

John looked at Celest and said, "I know you won't do it. You're way too stubborn for that." Celest seemed to be on the point of action. Slowly, she raised her right hand. As she closed it, the solid case of earth that now held a sleeping Eric climbed up over his head and sealed him inside.

The siren broke into hysterical laughter, "My power is supreme!"

Celest turned to the siren and said, "Something funny? What do you think you're laughing at?"

The stone case exploded open and a sixty foot tall, stone gorilla stood glaring at the evil siren. In her surprise, the siren let her grip on Kevano slip and he got away. Wasting no time, Eric fell upon the siren and pounded her into a dark memory. With his task completed, Eric turned back into his happy, and much smaller, self.

Above them the battle between Stormy and the ocean snake was still raging on. Both the wave-snake and Stormy were resting on the ocean's surface. Tsunami-like waves were being generated by the serpent. As they reached Stormy they were shredded by an invisible force field of wind. When the waves failed to kill Stormy, the serpent opened his mouth wide and sprayed his venom. Stormy easily dodged this attempt on his life and struck down the vile snake with two large bolts of lightning.

Once the fight was over, Stormy went back down to the ocean floor to see how the Windhearts were doing. Celest ran up to him and threw her arms around his neck, "You must be one of the best friends I've ever had! Even while you were busy with your fight you managed to find time to help me break free of the siren's control!" The reason Celest felt this way was because what other creature could communicate using peals of thunder. "I can't say thank you enough. I almost..." Stormy looked puzzled and nuzzled her shoulder before leading the way back to the now visible castle.

The second trip through the kingdom of Heaven's Mirror was much more pleasant than the first. The once gray and lifeless mer-people were now back to their colorful and joyous selves. There were countless warm faces thanking them for saving the kingdom from the Oblivion King's tyranny. Many of the mermen and mermaids wanted to go to the castle to pick up their children, and soon there was a large parade of parents following the Windheart's party to the castle.

Upon arriving at the castle they found King Ladagat waiting for them at the castle gates. Once they were in front of him he spoke, "Brave, noble heroes from the world beyond ours. You must have a reward for helping us out of such a dire situation. Firstly, the record I spoke of will be created and sealed away. Secondly, I grant you one quarter of the treasury. It is mostly rare pearls and gold coins. Please tell me where you would have me send it."

Celest shook her head and said, "You owe us nothing. We would have had to fight those monsters sooner or later because we're after Oblivion King. But thanks anyway."

King Ladagat looked impressed at her lack of greed as he marveled at her honesty. His elderly face seemed to radiate kindness and wisdom, "It is true that you would have had to beat them sooner or later. But that does not change the fact that we benefited from your hard work does it? Now allow us the honor of being gracious to our guests by allowing us to show our thanks. So, where shall I send the treasure to?"

Celest nodded her head and said, "If you really want to, would it be okay to have it sent to Rose Brew?"

Ladagat chuckled merrily and said, "Consider it done!

And now for my third suggestion, how about we have a grand celebration tonight?"

Eric smiled and John said, "I think Eric understands more than we give him credit for. But I agree with him. A party sounds like a lot of fun!"

The mer-king smiled and said, "Wonderful. Preparations are underway."

Celest walked up to him and shook his hand before saying, "Thanks, for everything."

That night they had a party that was by far the most unique celebration experience they ever had. The king had used his trident to make half of the banquet hall waterless. It seems that one of the Windhearts new found friends had overheard Celest talking about not wanting to eat underwater and had told the king. Terra prepared a banquet for the entire assembly, some eight hundred people, using some of the contents of the smallest bag. There were both foods from the Windheart's world and many of the new dishes that Celest had tried and loved which came from the world they were staying in at present. While the banquet was definitely a meal to remember, it was the dancing that would always stay in the Windhearts' dearest memories.

You see, the mer-folk have many interesting, intricate, and complex dances. Take that fact, and add in the delightful color scheme their tales create. Not to mention the fact that they are not limited to the floor as we are. Perhaps you can see why this was a dance that they would remember for the rest of their lives.

The party lasted all night and the children all fell

asleep in the dry side of the banquet hall. It was the mer-songs that finally swept them off to dreamland. The music brought to Celest and her brothers dreams of rushing waters and dazzling sunlit skies. In the morning the king told them of a land to the south that possibly needed their help. He told them that it was from the south that the siren usually came from. So after they added some sup-plies to their bags, they said their goodbyes and headed south.

REUNITED

The water became so clear at times that the little group of proven heroes sometimes forgot that they were under the ocean at all. At these points, they could see the sky above them, and it was full of the type of fluffy clouds that were ideal for imagination games. The games in which anyone with an imagination could see different animals and other shapes like planes, cars, bikes, buildings, and many other things that come to mind.

An hour or so before they reached the shore, the dark guard with a sunrise colored tail, caught up with them and said, "Hey, if it's alright with you, I would like to represent the kingdom of Heaven's Mirror in your battle with the Oblivion King. I know you've seen my wife demonstrating her skills while teaching her dry land class. I've got all her skills and advanced combat skills to top things off." Celest noticed that on each of his hands were a set of brass knuckles.

She smiled and said, "Ms. Serena is your wife? She

seems like a nice lady. Are you sure you want to risk her ending up alone, Mister…?"

The merman smiled, "The name is Desmond Obadiah. And it was my wife who suggested to the king that I come to help in the first place."

After consulting with her companions, Celest decided to allow Desmond to join the party. It was Terra who said, "When facing a foe like the Oblivion King, one should be thankful for any help that may be sent their way."

With that matter decided, they continued their underwater journey toward land. Once they had reached shore, a horrible situation awaited them. They met a large group of Ratadda warriors and some of the reptilian eyed, ebon clad, masked monsters that had earlier tried to slay Iron Back. As frightening as these adversaries were, the darkness knight leading them was far worse. Oddly enough, Celest no longer felt any animosity toward him. Well, at least not as much as she did before. After John had told Celest about what he saw beneath the armor, she simply wanted to stop him. She knew that it was Oblivion King that was her true enemy.

The party split up and began to rage war with their assailants. Early on in the fight two of the reptilian monsters cornered Eric and he began throwing rocks and such at them. They laughed maliciously as they dodged all his attacks. His siblings and friends would have been there to help protect him, but at the moment they were trying to both finish off the fight quickly and not die in the process.

After throwing a few unsuccessful kicks and punches, Eric grew frustrated and chucked his headband at one of the evil little beasts. It connected and knocked the creature out. At that moment, the other beast he was facing pricked Eric's shoulder with his sword before running off to help his allies. Eric did not seem to be too bothered by his wound. It was just a tiny one after all.

He was running toward Stormy when the evil knight blocked his path. Wicked laughter came from deep inside the armor. It brought up its enormous pitch black sword and aimed at Eric with a downward stroke. Before it made contact, Celest jumped between them and held up her elemental heart. The knight's sword was caught in a whirlwind. Though it seemed that Celest had foiled his attack, the knight continued to laugh. He pressed his twelve foot long broad sword down and Celest began to buckle. Suddenly she felt strength surging through her body. She looked down at her right leg to see Eric holding on to it while giving the darkness knight dirty looks from behind her. Just beyond the knight, Celest saw John diving at a ratadda solider.

After pecking and clawing at its face John called to Celest, "Remember his shoulder!"

Celest wasted no time. Using the burst of strength Eric had given her she threw the knight back and off balance. She then leapt high into the air toward the knight's right shoulder. As she flew toward him, three bolts of lightning extended out of the storm stone at the tip of her elemental heart. They wove themselves into a long blade of lightning and she plunged it into the hidden monster. In a puff of gray smoke, the armor crumbled and the elfin boy fell slowly to the ground. Upon seeing their commander fall, the group of dark creatures fled. It was a very intense and frightening moment. For at that instant both Terra and Oscar let out screams.

Terra ran toward the boy yelling, "Oh my God! Alex!" The others ran to Oscar who was standing beside a pale and unconscious Eric.

Oscar leaned over to check his pulse, "Still alive. Where is the gift I gave him? It would have protected him. The swords that the masked monsters use are forged from their fangs. Those beasts are called Alokans. They are highly poisonous!" John rushed away to find his brother's head band. Once he found it, he brought it back and dropped it at Oscar's feet. Oscar shook his head sadly, "Well done, but…it can only *prevent* poisoning. It does not cure it." Everyone, including Desmond, began to weep. Terra walked up to them with her own eyes red. She had already been weeping with joy at being reunited with her son.

She calmly asked, "Why is everyone just standing around? Eric needs help."

Oscar looked up at her and replied, "I don't have the power to heal him." Oscar was appalled to see that Terra was smiling.

She shrugged her shoulders and said, "Yes, *you* don't have the power to heal him." She turned to Celest, "Please go into one of the bags and get me one of the getveable roots."

Celest looked as if she had just drank an eight-gallon bottle of pure hope. She said "Why didn't I think of that?" before leaping up and scurrying into the medium sized bag. Once Celest got back she gave it to Terra who took the root and placed its tip against Eric's wound. It slowly turned a vivid shade of purple before withering and falling to the ground. Oscar returned Eric's headband to his head. Terra leaned down to kiss his forehead before asking the others to follow her.

She led them all to her weeping son and said, "This is Alex. I thought he was dead, but he was alive and Celest and Eric saved him!" Terra kneeled down and hugged her weeping boy.

He sobbed, "Mom, Dad is dead and I think I am the reason. What if I was the one who…?" Terra blanched slightly but then shook her son and said firmly, "No, if anything is responsible for the death of your dad it is Oblivion King." In the distance Alex's sword was changing. Not in size, but in color. It was as if the sword were shedding a suffocating cocoon. The blackness cracked and crumbled to the earth like the evil armor did when Celest destroyed the monster within. Instead of the cursed darkness sword, it was a highly polished sword with a pearl handle inlayed with gold filigree that rested in the sand. It seemed to be illuminating the beach they were on with silver light.

Terra looked from the sword to her son and said, "Get a hold of yourself, get your sword, and let's get going. Sorry, but we have no time to waste." Celest watched as Alex went over to get his weapon.

She asked Terra, "But that thing is huge. How could anyone other than a giant use it?"

Terra smiled, "That is an elfin sword in its true form. Alex will be able to use it effectively for two reasons. The first thing you should know is that sword was a coming of age gift to Alex from both my uncle and my husband. My husband is…was a renowned sword smith. With permission from my uncle, he sealed one of his branches inside one of the finest blades he ever made. The sword became a living thing which would only allow one of our bloodline to use it. It also displays the qualities my uncle does.

So in essence, it hates evil, honors those pure of heart, and is loyal to family. If anyone outside our family tried to use it, it would make itself so heavy that even someone with the strength of fifty full grown mountain giants would not be able to lift it. The second is the fact that Alex is an elfin warrior. As such, he could easily use a two hundred pound sword. His sword has many hidden powers. One of them causes it to weigh less than a pound when he uses it, unless he wills other wise, so all his sword techniques become that much more devastating."

Celest looked at the gigantic broad sword in awe, "You mean that sword is a part of 'Smith'? That is so cool!"

Terra laughed as Alex shouldered his great sword and returned to the rest of the party. Desmond shook Alex's free hand, "I'm glad to meet you. I just heard about that sword of yours, amazing."

Terra turned to Desmond, "Where shall we go now?"

Desmond pointed to the southwest and said, "There is a village in that direction. Humans mostly. I think we should go there."

So they all did. While they were walking John noticed that while none of Alex's emotions had left him, he grew quiet and seemed to put on a mask of cool confidence. John was pretty sure that was how Alex would act under any circumstance but still felt sorry for him. How could anyone "act like themselves" when they felt the way John knew Alex still did. Terra expressed regret as she told Desmond of how she wished they did not leave her glider behind when entering the lake. Celest checked Eric's wound again, not at all comfortable with the fact that her little brother was hurt. Once they reached the village, Terra told her son to go with the rest of the party to speak with the village chieftain. In the meantime, she and Celest stopped by a shop to see if there were any supplies they might need.

Fading Ignorance,
Blossoming Love

The shop keeper was a portly man with a frayed mustache and beard. Terra was looking around when she came across some climbing equipment and well-made tents that she liked very much. Terra smiled and said to Celest, "You never know when things like these will come in handy." She placed them neatly on the counter to purchase them.

The shop keeper's eyes nearly popped out of his head as he turned to Celest. "I do not serve her kind. Find another store." Terra looked shocked but only for a moment.

She quietly said, "My kind? Well, if you have no use for *my* money then I should be on my way. Good day."

Celest was so angry that her eyes filled with unshed tears. All Celest could think of was how kind, gentle, and caring Terra had been to her and her brothers since they had met. She did not understand what this fat little man meant by *her kind*. The man began to shout, "Now get out of my store, elf!" The invisible dam within Celest's eyes gave way and hot angry tears spilled down her face. Celest's hand went to her weapon but only found Terra's hand holding it on the spot.

Terra looked down at Celest and said, "Think, what would you accomplish by doing this? Attacking the man would only make things worse and bring you to his level. Imagine if I lashed out against him. Do you think that would snuff out his hatred towards elves? Or would it add fuel to his misguided and consuming hate? No, at times like these it is best to be on our best behavior. We cannot force people like these to see that we're people too, but we can *show* them. Some will come around and others will not. Just be thankful for the ones that do. Because it was once said that 'there are none so blind as those who will not see' and the ones who continue to hate fall among this group of people, they are to be pitied. Let's go."

Celest threw the man a last contemptuous glance before allowing herself to be led by the hand out of the shop. As they left, two men with crude pistols went passed them into the shop saying, "We will steal what we can and then skip town."

As they opened the door and went inside Terra sighed and said to Celest, "Stay out here please. I will be out soon." Celest watched in confusion as Terra went to help the man that had been so rude to her. Terra pushed the door to the shop open. As she stepped into the shop the taller of the two turned to Terra grinning wickedly.

"Look what we have here. An elf coming into a shop like she belongs in this land! Have you forgotten the last time your ilk faced us humans in war?"

Terra shook her head, "I was not around for this war

you are so proud of. Since my people fled from such horrific displays long ago, I have been taught that there are no victors in war only death."

The smaller robber snorted, "Spoken like a true coward. Typical."

Terra sighed, "I would ask you to please leave this man and his shop in peace. It is not right for you to take what you did not earn."

The criminals looked to one another in disbelief. The taller of the two shrugged and pointed his pistol at Terra who was still standing beside the door. Anticipating his treachery, and the trajectory of his bullet, she gracefully sidestepped the attack. She then took a stance from an ancient elfin martial art which had been taught to her by her grandfather.

Terra asked sadly as she readied herself, "Is there no other way?" The thieves both fired again and hit the wall where she once stood. Terra flowed gracefully around the room gliding around their attacks like a river glides over the small stones in its bed. Soon they were out of ammunition and found her standing right in front of them. Terra gave them both a half smile, "I tried to warn you." She knocked them out with precise blows as overwhelming as an avalanche, before restraining them with a rope from a nearby shelf. Terra turned to the shaken shop keeper. "Call what authorities you may have." The keeper looked at her through new eyes.

The first result of this confrontation was that the man reconsidered his view point. The other was that he gave Terra the supplies she had wanted to purchase earlier free of charge. When they caught up with the others, Terra showed them the climbing equipment and told them how it could be used once they got to Oblivion King's castle. They would climb up a wall rather than force entry through the front gate. Stealth would be the plan as long as they could use it.

In turn the others told Celest and Terra about another and much larger dark knight that was rumored to be coming to the village that they had just arrived at. The village's name was Wolf's Peak. The *true* dark knight's name was Pathos, and he served as Oblivion King's head general. He was the only one, other than the dark king himself, that the ice dragon was forced to answer to.

That night they stayed in one of the village's inns. Alex had troubled dreams, and somehow felt that if he did not destroy this knight on his own that he would go insane. Waking from a dream, in which he was the one who killed his dad, he got out of bed and went outside for a walk. Celest could not sleep either so she got up and did the same. The reason that Celest could not sleep was that she kept wondering what would happen to their mom if she and her brothers failed. Celest and Alex ran into each other somewhere outside. Desmond watched them from the roof of the inn.

Celest smiled, "So how's it going? Can't sleep either, huh?"

Alex shrugged, "Guess not. You know, my mom thinks really highly of you. She says that you are much like my sword, powerful and pure."

Celest shook her head. "No, I'm not that powerful. My family and friends give me strength. The only time I feel strong on my own is when I have to protect them...my brothers, Stormy, your mom, or Oscar."

Alex nodded, "That makes sense. It works that way for

elves and other creatures too." Celest recalled what had happened earlier that day, "Yeah, we're all the same. We all have emotions and can think for ourselves. It is so stupid that some people can't see that! Earlier today the man in the shop would not sell your mom what she wanted just for being an elf."

Alex shook his head, "Humans have a lot of nerve for being such frail creatures."

Celest grew indignant, "You should never stereotype! I'm a human. Do you think you could hang with me?"

Alex grew silent and looked ashamed of himself. "If my mom or my dad could have heard what I just said... I'm sorry. To be honest, no I don't think I could. My mom told me how you beat the ice dragon. Since he captured me and my dad and you scattered him to the wind, it is safe to say that you would defeat me."

Celest was taken back by his honesty and felt less angry, "Sorry I got mad. Your mom is a strong, smart, and nice woman. Mine is too, so like I said we are all the same."

Alex smiled, "Yeah. I guess we are."

As the two went inside Desmond smiled to himself, "How sweet it is when a simple truth is uncovered." Below him, inside the inn, no one noticed Terra watching Celest and her son through the window. She looked very sad. You see, Terra could sense the possibility of love in the air. When she was growing up, she heard of many situations in which a mortal fell in love with one of the timeless. These romances never ended well. One would grow old and pass away while the other would live forever only to mourn the gaping emptiness he or she felt in their heart.

Terra sighed and went back to bed saying to herself,

"Well, if anyone is worth risking that type of pain for, I guess it would have to be someone like Celest."

Blade of Autumn

The next morning Alex told everyone that he had to face Pathos alone. If any of Pathos' allies joined in he had no problem accepting help, but Pathos was to be his and his alone. They all turned to Terra to ask her opinion, "We will let him fight it out on his own, but if it looks as if the monster is going to kill my son we will destroy it ourselves." Alex looked like he was going to say something to the contrary, but he was silenced by a look from Terra before she said, "I will not lose you twice."

Desmond raised his hand and said, "I also have a request. You see, before now you've had to do all the work. I know it won't catch me up, but I would like it if you'd kindly leave any minions of this Pathos guy for me."

Celest nodded, "All right, but the same applies. If it looks as though you need our help, we won't hesitate. Sound good?" Desmond smiled and nodded his approval.

They did not have to wait for Pathos for very long. The next day he showed up with about fifty Alokans. In a thunderous voice he shouted, "Pay my king tribute and I might not destroy you. Defy me, and you will beg for death long before I give it to you." Oscar, Terra, the Windhearts, and Stormy waited on the roof of the village's clock tower and watched. Below them Alex and Desmond walked straight up to their foes.

Alex laughed coldly, "You *might* not destroy them. How kind of you. Hey, Desmond you ready?" In response, the same neon sparks that appear when Desmond's wife does a star-runner technique, filled the air around him before being sucked into both his feet and his fists. In the flash of an eye Desmond was suddenly standing back to back with three alokans who promptly fell to the ground. Alex smiled, "Glad to hear it. Now, Pathos." Alex said nothing else but pointed his great sword at the towering dark knight. Although the difference in size between Pathos and Alex was insane, their swords were about the same size. Alex jumped into the air and high above the ground their swords clashed. Clang, clang, clang, *shing*. Alex landed and his eyes seemed to radiate an indefinable fire.

Pathos roared with laughter, and spoke even as he and Alex fought, "We seem to be equally matched. Once the ice dragon brought you and your father to me; I thought you might prove to be of some use. So straight away I spell bound you, got one of my goblins and placed you both into a suit of my enchanted armor. Your dad tried to stop me. He was a magnificent sword master and nearly killed me, but you proved to be as useful as I thought you'd be. You blocked his finishing blow. It was wonderful! You gave me the opening I needed to finish him off!" Alex roared in anger and knocked the dark knight onto his back. Pathos continued to laugh, "Your dad died because of your weak mind! You could not resist my power. You should be dead instead of him!"

Alex's face fell, "Perhaps you're right. But, I *am* still alive and my dad's death *will not* be in vain!" Alex whispered to his sword, "Autumn Edge!" Although he whispered, his voice seemed to reverberate throughout the whole village. Alex once again leaped high into the air and swung his sword from left to right. As he did so, a whirlwind of silver leaves soared toward the dark general. Upon collision, the leaves exploded into golden flame. The evil knight was lost to that inferno. Just as Alex was finishing off the knight, Desmond was dropping the last two alokans.

He turned to Alex, "We did it!"

But Alex did not hear him. He had fallen to his knees and was weeping once again, "Father, I am sorry. It was because of me that you needed avenging in the first place."

Before the group went on to continue their journey, Terra asked if it would be alright if they returned to Rose Brew so that she could take the memorial she built for Alex down. Everyone could see how important it was to her, so they all agreed at once that Rose Brew was their next destination. When they arrived Terra prepared a wonderful dinner. Terra began their miniature banquet with soup. It was rich and creamy. The closest thing to it that the Windhearts had tasted was a smoked Gouda soup. Next she brought out thin strips of beef that had been fried in a salty but sweet brown sauce, and vegetables that were battered with a crisp coating of seasoned flour. To drink was zana. It was apparent that Terra wanted everyone to enjoy her son's first dinner back home. For dessert, Terra had baked a large assortment of pies. Everyone stayed up late talking, laughing, and joking. It was not until Eric had fallen asleep at the table that Terra called an end to the festivities and put everyone to bed. Alex slept in his old room downstairs, while everyone else went upstairs to the rooms they had stayed in before.

Before they went to sleep, Celest went outside to say goodnight to Stormy. Although Celest and her brothers knew that they were fighting to *get* home and to save their mother, in some way they felt like they had come home already when they arrived in Rose Brew. It had become their home away from home. The Windhearts had faced many dangers up until this point. Each seeming worse than the last, but with their new found friends, the children felt like nothing was impossible. As long as they had each other nothing had enough dark power to keep them from their world, and especially from their mother.

The next morning they woke up around eight. After a hearty breakfast, Terra led them to the memorial site. She had brought a large sledgehammer and broke Alex's memorial into tiny chunks of granite. With the last few blows her eyes filled with tears. She turned to her husband's memorial. It was tall, covered with flowers and elfin lettering exquisitely carved into its surface. The monument translated, "In loving memory of my husband Charles. Till the day I join you, I will mourn you. Forever your wife, Terra.'" She stood on the spot for a long moment. It looked as if she longed to break down her husband's stone as well. Dropping her hammer she covered her face with both hands and began to weep. Alex and the Windhearts gathered around her and simply held her. Oscar patted her on the shoulder, and Stormy nuzzled her. No one said anything. There are times when words cannot convey even a quarter of what a simple touch can.

Later that day, back at Terra's home, Celest asked Oscar why the memorial did not have Terra's husband's last name on it. He smiled slightly and said, "From what I gather, a last name is something that is passed on so that when that person dies, a part of him lives on. For the timeless, their blood being shared with their children is enough. The name they go by is the one that will likely 'live' forever. So to us, we have little use for last names." Celest still looked like her question was not completely answered.

"That makes a lot of sense. But, you guys can still die. So why not use last names?"

Oscar stood for a moment admiring her way of thinking before saying, "It is true that we can die. But, we choose to think on the positive and assume that if we are careful enough we can avoid death. Even if we do die, our children are a nearly eternal monument of the fact that we did indeed once exist." Celest looked like the topic was depressing her, but she also looked satisfied with the answer Oscar had given her. Oscar could see that Celest was beginning to feel a little upset. Changing the subject, Oscar gave her a gentle smile, "Terra said that tomorrow she is going to take you to see 'Smith.' I, for one, look forward to learning his real name. Just think about this, Terra said that one day she will tell your story. Elves are great at remembering things like that. You and your brothers are already living legends! I have to go and send a message to

Marlene. It has been a while since we have been able to speak." Excusing himself, Oscar went upstairs and sent one of his orbs of golden light through the open window.

The next day came quickly enough, and Terra woke them all bright and early. Taking the lead, she brought the others two miles to the east of the village and then across a great canyon. About six feet from the other side was a huge tree. Its bark was silvery brown and its leaves were a golden green. It had many long and powerful branches. Two limbs stood out isolated from the rest. One was pointed toward a large rock away from the canyon and the other was hanging a little over the side. The branch hanging over the side of the canyon had three very thin, rough looking scars around its middle. Terra smiled and said, "I would like you to meet my uncle! Celest, I believe you had a question."

Celest stepped forward and said, "Terra has told me and my brothers your story. She thought that it would be better for me to ask you your name myself, so in the story she called you 'Smith.' Could you please tell me what your real name is?" For a while it looked as if the answer would not come.

After a while longer a soft breeze blew through the leaves of the great tree, and it began to whisper, "My name is Oren. No need to tell me your names. The winds have already brought me news of your exploits. Young Celest, John, and Eric Windheart it is nice to finally meet you all."

Celest smiled, "Oren, it is a very nice name. Glad to meet you, too."

Terra turned to the group. "My uncle cannot see. When he became a tree he lost all of his senses but the ability to hear. He does know, however, what is going on all around the world. As he said, the winds bring him news." Terra looked up at the great tree, "Uncle Oren is Oblivion King's barrier down now? Will we be able to get through?" They had to wait for a while before Oren answered. They had to wait for another breeze.

When it came Oren whispered, "The barrier is now very weak, gaping holes open in it from time to time. With good timing you could indeed get through."

Desmond laughed, "Great news! I'll be home with my wife in no time at all!"

As another breeze caressed them, Oren added, "Perhaps not as soon as you think. You see, within the barrier is first a marshland filled with acid. They refer to it as Darkness Tears Swamp. Next is a labyrinth-like forest filled with the worst kind of monsters imaginable. Although, it was not always such a horrid place, no it was once very pleasant. The princess of Dawn's Sweet Dew fell in love with the prince of Dusk Wind. Their kingdoms were always at war with each other...and also at war with anyone who came too close to their lands. Tired of all the fighting, Princess Elena and Prince Bryan eloped and went off to the Sacred Forest in order to start their own humble kingdom. Upon their arrival they were happy to find a castle already built. Little did they know the dark and tragic history that befell the kingdom so long ago.

The occupants of their kingdom were mostly the magical creatures that lived there before Bryan and Elena had arrived. They were happy to have wise and kindhearted rulers once again. But in the hearts of the most ancient creatures was an underlying fear that old tragedies were waiting to repeat themselves.

Without the rightful heirs, their home kingdoms could not continue with their war. Without the prince and princess, the kingdoms would simply cease to be, according to their old laws. This proved to be bad news for a certain dark wizard by the name of Jakaroe. You see, he was selling dark weapons to both sides. He tried to bring back the prince and princess, but Prince Bryan was an exquisite archer and felled him with a single shot from his bow the moment he saw the dark wizard approaching the castle gates. At the time, Oblivion King only needed a little more power to break free from his luminous prison. Before Jakaroe died, he cursed the newborn kingdom with all the darkness that had consumed his humanity. Oblivion King thrived on such foolishness. You see, it was the dark wish of a certain man that brought Oblivion King into existence. His name was William. He was a man whose pain was healed only by the love of his family. It then returned seven fold when he had everything he loved torn away from him. The pain he felt after losing all he cherished created darkness so intense that no light was thought strong enough to penetrate it. He wished for all things to be brought to nothingness, but only after tasting the bitter pain he died with.

So you see, Oblivion King was more than happy to feed on the ill intent of yet another spiteful being. Using the evil energy Jakaroe generated, the Oblivion King took his freedom. As a side effect, the dark wizard's wish was also granted. But, he only did so because it suited his own dark purpose. Even before the kingdom was given a name, it was destroyed. The sacred forest became the

Forgotten Forest, and within its dark depths lies the castle whose walls once sheltered William and his family. It now stands as Oblivion King's stronghold, and it is there that he awaits you. But have no fear. The winds from ancient times have brought stories of hope. They tell me that there is an answer that is likened to a flower waiting to bloom. Perhaps the young Windhearts are the answer to his darkness. Do not get complacent. You still have your work cut out for you."

They stayed in Rose Brew for another few weeks. The time was spent mostly on hard training. Desmond sparred with Terra. They were incredibly well matched, they both moved so quickly and attacked so accurately that they seemed to be dancing a fast pace ballet. A stranger sight was when Oscar and Alex tested their sword skills against one another. Oscar looked like a tiny spec next to Alex's twelve foot sword. None the less, Oscar put Alex through his paces. Oscar knocked him off balance several times, and while he did so he gave him advice on how to improve his performance. Alex was not offended in the slightest. As he was just a little over fourteen and Oscar was hundreds of years his senior, he took the advice with a thankful heart. And his skills improved greatly because of it. The Windhearts practiced with each other, even Eric. Their powers and their control grew by an astonishing amount. In fact, their powers grew so much that about twice as much of their abilities now spilled over into each other. Celest was twice as strong, and her sight became twice as sharp. John was also stronger and more at ease with the various elements. Eric, although he could not tell anyone, was more resistant to the elements and his sight also improved. Stormy was the only one who did not train; his own abilities being mastered thousands of years ago. Terra restocked the packs and the Windhearts were soon saying goodbye to their second home, the beautiful village, Rose Brew.

Journey to the
Black Citadel

Before heading to the Oblivion King's palace they stopped by the lake near Bulaklak Haven to pick up Terra's glider. It would be a much more comfortable trip with it due to their needing more room to accommodate Desmond and Alex. Once they had the glider they were on their way. The sun rose, set, and had finished rising again before it suddenly vanished from the sky. They had reached the Oblivion King's domain and the enchanted night that engulfed it. The field of darkness which surrounded the dark king's castle and grounds seemed to be unstable. Every now and then the field would break and you could see a gap where the darkness seemed to be less solid. It was in these places that there seemed to be the faintest glimmer of twilight in the air.

After they landed, they left the glider behind and went through one of the shifting gaps. Beyond the dark field a great river surrounded the castle, Darkness Tears Swamp, and the Forgotten Forest. After they had crossed the river, the acidic marsh rested in front of them reflecting only darkness. Alex was just about to walk ahead when Celest threw her arm out in front of him. She looked at him and said, "Don't you remember?"

Alex looked back and shrugged his shoulders, "No. What's the matter?" Celest said nothing. Instead she reached down and picked up a rock and dropped it right on the edge of the marsh. The marsh around the rock fizzed slightly and the rock was no more. Alex looked from the spot where the rock had once been and looking embarrassed he smiled at Celest. "Thanks. Training must have pushed the fact that the swamp was acidic right out of my head. Good catch."

The marsh was huge. Terra suggested that they fly over it, but Oscar shook his head, "Do you see any bats, birds, or even insects flying around over the marsh? I think that the fumes coming up off the acid make it impossible to breath in the air above it." Celest looked around.

It was after her eyes fell on the river that she turned to John, "Are you thinking what I'm thinking?"

John nodded, "Ready when you are."

She pointed her elemental heart at John. Water splashed out of its tip and wrapped itself around him. Soon John was obscured by a giant ball of water. After a few moments the water fell to the earth and John was hovering in the air in front of Celest. He had become a bird of flowing water. He was about the same size that he was when he had become the firebird. Only now his eyes were blue spheres that seemed to be deeper than the ocean. His feathers were long and flowing. It looked like they were going to pour off of his body but never did.

Celest patted him on the beak and smiled, "Well, get to it." John nodded and flew toward the river. Once he reached it, he turned abruptly and flew directly back toward the swamp. It seemed as if all the water in the river wanted to aid John and his siblings; it had left its bed and now followed John in the form of a great wave. As he reached the swamp's edge, John flew straight up toward the blackened sky to allow the wave to pass under him.

As the wave dragged all of the acid back into the river Desmond shouted, "Good Job! You and your siblings are truly amazing!" Terra and Eric walked up to John to pat him on his beak. As they touched him, he lowered his head. His feathers actually did pour off of his body as he turned back into a golden eagle. His eyes were full of happiness as he looked up at Terra and his brother. He fluttered over to Celest to sit on her shoulder. Together they walked across the stony ground where the acid had once been. Soon the Forgotten Forest stood in front of them with all of its dark greenery.

As they entered into yet another strange forest, Celest could not shake the feeling that the forest was more than just alive with animals and other creatures. No, somewhere deep inside, she knew that the forest itself was alive with evil. She could feel it breathing.

Desmond rubbed his knuckles in anticipation as he said, "It's kind of funny how evil monsters like the Oblivion King always seem to find places like this to live in." Eric's eyes darted about as they began to walk along a path that seemed to appear out of nowhere. On a number of occasions, while still inside the forest, John could swear that he could hear the trees talking to one another. He even thought that he saw them slowly creeping around some times. Shortly before John told Celest this unpleasant fact, she told him that a couple of times she could hear the trees jeering them behind their backs. John ruffled his feathers uncomfortably as he sat on her shoulder. Celest was very comforting to both of her brothers. John felt safe there on her shoulder, and Eric felt safe as long as his sister had him by the hand. All of the trees seemed to be draped in cobwebs. As they approached a dead and slimy looking bush they could hear labored breath coming from behind it.

Both Oscar and Alex held their blades at the ready as Desmond called to the thing behind the bush, "If you are hurt maybe we can help, but if you are an enemy beware."

After a few seconds a gray haired man came out from behind the bush, "Get out of here now. You're not welcome! Is it not enough that I have been abandoned by my family? That dark king messed up my life and now you're here to make it worse? *Leave an old man alone!*"

Oscar did not lower his sword as he replied to the man's self-pitying statements, "But you are not an old man are you? Do not think that I do not see you for what you truly are, werewolf."

The creature's face broke out into a grin exposing long canines and said in his wheezy voice, "What if I am? I have no interest in dealing with the likes of you. My only concern is my pack and how that monster took their loyalty from me, *their leader*, with all of his hollow promises and his deceptions. But you, what is your business here?"

Oscar responded again, "Not that it is any of your business, but we are here to destroy the dark king."

A very cunning look spread across the old werewolf's face, "Well now, that would prove most convenient for me. It was because of that beast that my own pack mauled me. I'll tell you what. On the path ahead a fork of sorts is awaiting you. I could just tell you which way, but you are still no friends of mine. Instead, I'll tell you that the Camp of Honesty is your best bet. I will also tell you that of the two *things* that await you, only one of them speaks the truth. He is from the camp you need. The other is a compulsive liar. Should you make the mistake of heading into his Village of Deception, you will be snuffed out like candles. You may ask them one question, or one request and they will respond in turn. I'd wish you luck but..."

With that said the old man turned into a gray wolf and bounded off into the darkness. His breath still ragged. They continued to walk along the path as the group at large wondered if there was any truth to the old wolf's words. After a time they did reach a fork in the road. It was also true that it was guarded by two creatures. One was a Minotaur with long deadly horns. The other seemed to be made of swamp sludge, dead twigs, and leaves. At once, everyone began to discuss what they had considered in the time between meeting the werewolf and arriving on the spot where they now stood. Could the wolf be trusted?

Terra shook her head in an agitated fashion, "Well it seems that he was telling us the truth so far. But, what are we going to ask them?" They all stood there for a moment making suggestions.

Out of the blue, Celest laughed out loud, "It is so simple! No wonder it's so hard to figure out. The question seems hard so we try to make up a hard solution to go with it." Not elaborating she walked over to the two monsters and said, "Please, take us to your camp." Stormy walked up to Celest and nuzzled her in approval of her quick and intelligent mind. Alex and Desmond actually laughed until they were winded. They were astounded by how simple the answer really was. The liar would take them to the honest camp, and the honest one would do the honest thing and take them to his own camp.

As they entered into a little forest clearing they could see many tents that seemed to be woven out of black silk. And as they reached the camp itself an unlikely pair of creatures approached them, an earthen gnome and a water goblin.

The gnome asked the travelers in a dry and tired voice, "What brings you to our camp?"

The goblin said in a watery and boiling voice, "Are you enemy or friend?"

Terra replied shortly, "I do not know about 'friend,' but perhaps allies. You see we are here to destroy Oblivion King."

The creatures looked surprised for a moment. The gnome shook his head slightly while grinning to himself. "I see, good luck on that endeavor, you'll need it."

The goblin ran off into the nearest tent as the gnome continued to speak, "Well, the enemy of my enemy is my friend. If you venture on ahead you will meet up with dark trees. They are large and will block your path. If you try to go around them, you will find that they will simply move in front of you again. As fast as you are, they will always move faster." The goblin came running out of the tent and handed a horn which seemed to be carved out of a very hard, black wood to Alex.

After he handed over the horn he said, "There will be times when you encounter these trees. Blow the horn and they will freeze on the spot for at least ten minutes. But make sure you blow it every five minutes when you are around these monstrous trees. You don't want to lose track of time and have them moving about again, especially if you have already had gotten passed them. The dark trees can get violent and hate it when they fail to block the path of those they consider intruders."

Celest looked at the gnome asking, "Why does this horn have that effect on the trees here?"

The gnome laughed and said, "It was carved out of the tree that started off their existence in the first place." The instant the gnome spoke these words Alex's sword began to pulsate with silver light. The dark horn began to resonate with the same silver light as darkness poured out of the horn's mouth piece. Seconds later, the horn was a golden color and Alex's sword was still once again.

The gnome gasped and said, "How did you return the horn to its original state? That is the color the dark trees once had before the Oblivion King warped them. Now the horn will not freeze them, it will restore them!"

Alex shrugged and said, "My sword is also part of a tree, but a good one." The goblin went up to Alex to shake his hand but Alex simply looked away.

Celest looked from Alex to the goblin and said, "Sorry, he had a very bad experience with a goblin. But I wonder if he remembers our conversation outside the inn. Stereotyping, you can't judge an entire people by the actions of one person. "

Alex looked at Celest for a moment and then turned to the goblin and shook his hand, "Sorry, I know all goblins are not the same. But in my defense, one did shove darkness down my throat while I was under an enchantment."

The goblin looked sad as he replied, "I understand… so…it was you who killed Gahald. Well he deserved it, I suppose."

Celest felt bad for him and sighed. "No, it was me who did it. Please believe me when I say I am sorry, but I really had no choice."

The goblin smiled weakly, "Pity for a goblin? You're not at all like the dark one, are you? You should head on now. Good luck."

CREATURES OF DARKNESS

They all thanked the goblin and gnome for the horn and followed the path that lead out of the opposite side of the village. As they walked along the new path Celest thought about how much worse this forest was than the JaPoyPoy forest. At least in the JaPoyPoy forest they started out with *some* sunlight. In the Forgotten Forest they started out with barely any light at all, and soon all the light they had was just a sort of half twilight. At any rate, the group walked for a long time before coming upon six gigantic trees. Their bark was as dark as midnight, and the fruit on their limbs were a poisonous red. They tried to walk past but the trees blocked their way. No matter which way they ran the dark trees continued to deny their passage. Alex put the horn to his lips. The note that rang out as a result shook the air, and the nearest tree changed back into its old self. It was the same color of the horn with deep green leaves. The other trees tried to attack the heroes by pelting them with their heavy fruits, but the tree that Alex had revived began to swat them back toward the dark assailants. Wasting no time, Alex darted from tree to tree while dodging lethal branches and hard-hitting fruits. He stopped at each one blowing the horn and restoring them to their original forms. Soon Celest and the others were able to pass without having to destroy the trees. The forest seemed to grow still darker with every step. If it had not been for John, the Windhearts would not have been able to see anything at all. Celest noticed that when the trees were restored to normal, some of the shadow folk darted ahead of them, and when Celest told Oscar this his face hardened.

"These shadow folk are probably not the curious type. No, they are probably rushing on ahead to tell Oblivion King that we got passed his twisted trees and are now heading his way. We had better hurry."

They continued down the path at a faster pace. As they reached the end of the forest, the castle of the Oblivion King towered high above them. Once they all had reached the castle gates a ghastly moaning sound filled the air. The hairs on the back of Celest's neck stood on end, and Eric turned around on the spot eyeing the forest with alarm and anger. John "looked" into the forest and saw that all of the life that once was hidden within that section of forest was gone. It had all been devoured by the old wizard's hatred. Slowly a large portion of the forest began to contract in on itself until it looked like a frightening blackish-green giant. It was the remnants of Jakaroe's hatred manifesting itself. His dark power remained although he had perished centuries ago.

At the monster's feet were the trees that Alex had revived just moments ago; they had been mulched. Alex and Desmond tried to attack the beast but were slapped to the ground and laid there quite still. Oscar darted around the monster slashing at it here and there but was unable to do sufficient damage. Stormy flew over to his fallen comrades, and took them to rest against the castle gate. Taking another approach, Oscar shot a fiery spark off his blade. The forest beast cringed back for an instant, and then he began to laugh as it pinched the spark between his index finger and thumb.

Terra noticed the beast's original reaction and called over to Celest, "It seems to be weak against fire, but you are the only one who can make one big enough to have a decent effect!" John was also watching the monster. He noticed that as soon as the spark was put out, the area around the wound closed in and healed the damaged foliage.

He turned to his sister and said, "You'll have to destroy it all at once, otherwise it will just get better again."

Celest nodded and held her elemental heart out to the side. As she had done earlier, she caused a long fiery whip to emerge from the tip. Celest cracked the whip twice in the air and then whipped it around the monster that had once been a part of the Forgotten Forest. It howled in pain and nearly jerked Celest off her feet, but she was a lot stronger now and held her ground. Eric tugged on her pant leg and Celest once again felt the surge of strength that she had earlier. She pulled down on her flaming whip causing the giant forest beast to fall. This made the ground shake so violently that everyone but Celest nearly fell over. She held it down as the fire totally destroyed it.

Once there was nothing left of the dark wizard's essence but ashes, Celest and the others went over to the castle gate where Terra was seeing to Desmond and Alex. She was bringing them back to a conscious state by using an ointment of lightning leaves. Soon after they were conscious they were also healed. As soon as they were ready to go, the group circled around the castle and used the climbing equipment Terra had attained earlier to scale the wall. No one noticed that as Desmond, who was the last in line, scrambled over the wall, the forest began to return to its once glorious and peaceful state. Once in the dark castle's courtyard a familiar face awaited them.

Celest shouted, "Iron Back!" and ran to his side. The powerful dragon was chained to a gigantic steel ring which was placed in the center of the courtyard, and was apparently lodged deep in the ground. Celest looked into Iron Back's face. His snout was wrapped in chain. Using her elemental heart, Celest created a large rock hammer and destroyed the chains that were holding him down. Once Iron Back's claws were free he reached up and snapped his chain muzzle. He looked tired and infuriated at the same time.

The ancient dragon turned to Celest once his mouth was free, "I will help you the best I can. The Oblivion King is using the body of what you would consider my cousin. Last I knew my cousin was on the verge of death, poisoned. Now I feel that I have an idea of *why* he was poisoned. He will not be able to rest in peace until he has been freed of the dark king. If only I were stronger. It's been a long time since I've eaten."

At these words Celest had an idea, "Terra, do we have any kaholoholo melons?"

Terra smiled, "The smallest pack has nothing but them in it. I thought that since this was going to be the roughest part of our journey we could use the extra nutrition and enjoy our favorite foods at the same time."

Celest whispered *awesome* before turning to Iron Back, "I would like for you to get inside the smallest bag here. I'd explain but I know that you can 'see' its charms. This is a way for you to enjoy the flavors you dragons like, without the guilt."

Iron Back smiled, "Smart girl. I see that you also saved that dark knight. Tell me, Alex, can you still shadow walk?"

Alex looked surprised, "That was always one of my abilities. And how is it that you know my name?"

Iron Back gave Alex a knowing smile and a rasping chuckle. He then turned back to Celest, "I shall take your advice. If you would like you could leave me and the pack here in the courtyard. The fight will likely end up here in the courtyard at any rate, judging by the size of my cousin, but maybe you should take me along. What do you think?"

Celest smiled, "I would like to have you with us, if you don't mind." Iron Back nodded and disappeared into the smallest pack.

With their reunited ally in tow, the heroic group headed into the dark palace. There were twists, turns, and many different monsters that hindered their path. The dark creatures included more goblins, regular sized trolls, gargoyles that were living statues of black marble, werewolves, giant scorpions, and every other manner of dark monster you could imagine. The Windhearts had already ample practice with their skills by this point. Not only that, but they wanted to get home to their mother so badly that they were slapping down the dark king's minions with a minimal effort.

The only creatures that posed any real difficulty to the Windhearts were the gargoyles of black marble. They were the true guardians of the Oblivion King's castle. It was in the castle's great hall that three of these monstrosities fell upon the Windhearts. Each one was at least as strong as Eric, and each so empowered by darkness that even John had trouble seeing them. Celest was the first to take one down. Time after time the dark gargoyle dived at her, slashing any part it could reach on Celest's body. She tried to fight back, but the monster was simply too fast. With each fresh attempt on her life, Celest's frustration grew. She was beginning to wonder what would happen to her family if the beastly monster managed to take her down. It was at that moment in time, when Celest felt like there was no way out, that a light seemed to go on in her head. The monster had swooped down on her and knocked Celest to the stone floor so often that she began to see a pattern. She quietly stood up, tiny trickles of blood dripping down her arms from the gashes that the gargoyle had left with its stony claws. As it dived at her for the last time, Celest leaped high into the air and came down on its back with her fist so hard that it crumbled into a big pile of rubble.

Eric also took a beating, but eventually he too had taken all that he could from the monster. He tore one of the castle's pillars out of the floor, and as the gargoyle came at him again he smashed it into a thousand pieces. John had the worst encounter with the gargoyles. He couldn't get a fix on the one assaulting him, each time he sent out a blast of his powerful golden light, the dark monster somehow managed to dodge it. Alex suddenly realized how the beast was doing it. The dark gargoyles could shadow walk just like he could. Celest saw that the gargoyle was about to drop the finishing blow. Her eyes widened with fear at the thought of losing her little brother.

Ignoring everything else, Celest felt her feet begin a mad dash to take her to help him. As she was running to his aid, Alex appeared out of nowhere in the air between John and the monster. Using *his* ability to shadow walk, Alex had instantly put himself in a position to attack. Alex split the gargoyle in two and as soon as he landed he mended John's wounds with lighting leaves. Celest was so happy that Alex saved John, that she threw her arms around her brother's hero. Alex looked awkward for a moment before freeing himself from her arms and tending to her wounds as well. Terra watched them from a distance as she patched Eric up.

Soon after encountering the dark gargoyles, they found themselves at the entrance to the castle's throne room. Before entering, Celest turned to her brothers, "If this monster is as evil and strong as I think, you are going to need this." She pointed her weapon at John and a giant fireball engulfed him. She turned it upon Eric and instead of the case of rock that enveloped him earlier; a stream of liquid steel sprayed and coated him. Moments later, where Celest's younger brothers once stood, a giant steel gorilla, and the firebird that had defeated the ice dragon, stared at her benevolently. Turning to everyone else she asked, "Are you ready?" Everyone nodded solemnly and turned to face the door.

Confronting the Darkness

The door splintered and grudgingly flew open as Celest's foot connected. They rushed into meet the dark king head on. Oblivion King was sitting on his throne. His blazing white eyes were the only truly visible part of his body. Out of the darkness surrounding his body the dark king sent out six colossal black fire balls. Everyone dodged out of their way and the fireballs took out a large portion of castle behind them. The Oblivion King rose up and flew out of the castle and into the courtyard. Once the monster landed he gave a deep roar and two giant griffons soared out from beyond the remains of the dark palace and landed in the courtyard. They snapped their beaks menacingly and began to charge Eric and John. The firebird and the steel gorilla waited for the beasts to approach. Their eyes burning with anticipation, but as the griffons were about to make contact, the little pack burst open and Iron Back emerged. It was amazing what the nutritious meal had done for him. His skin no longer clung to his bones but was tight against his revitalized muscles. He looked thick and strong. Iron Back blew fire at the griffons and they were forced away from John and Eric.

He shouted, "All of you must focus on Oblivion King! Leave these beasts to me!" Iron Back let out a deafening roar and rushed at the griffons taking the battle to the sky. Stormy in turn rushed Oblivion King, launching bolts of lightning. Celest caused a sword of fire to emerge from her elemental heart. She leaped at the evil king and slashed him. The dark monster roared in pain. The Oblivion King had been so busy avoiding Stormy's attacks that he did not notice Celest until it was too late. Alex and Desmond followed Stormy's lead and tried to distract the king so that the Windhearts could get a clean shot at him. Oscar and Terra stood by to protect the packs. As they had decided to be the medics in this battle, it was essential to keep the medical supplies out of harms way.

Eric was the one who found his opening next. He rushed in and punched the monster so hard that the Oblivion King went skidding across the ground, the dark aura around him beginning to weaken. At times they could see his entire scaly face. The fight continued to rage on. John soon found his opportunity and sent out a stream of twenty fireballs strafing him. The dark one staggered and continued to fight. Celest wove her way through Oblivion King's slashing claws dealing him another blow. Perhaps it was that her attacks hurt him the most because soon he began to focus his attention only on Celest. He launched a black fireball that was ten times bigger than anyone of his first six. It was too large for her to dodge, even with a portion of Eric's powers spilling into her. She braced herself for the worst. But the fire's cold heat suddenly faded.

Stormy was standing in front of her, steam rising up off of his body.

Celest smiled, "Thanks! You are really powerful to have saved me from *that*." Stormy's knees buckled and he fell to the ground. Celest's eyes widened in horror, as Terra and Oscar rushed to Stormy's side.

Celest's eyes started to sting and then tears began to stream down her face, "What's wrong with you! I know you could have let that attack pass straight through you! Why did you remain solid?" Celest never felt so afraid at seeing a storm roll out of her life.

Oscar looked up at Celest while the others continued to fight, "That is enough, he took the full force of that attack for one reason and one reason alone, he is your father. You know how your brothers changed form when they entered this world? When he entered yours he became a man, with time he learned to control the change. You are the children that the king wanted to destroy. The reason your dad has been absent from your life for so long is because he wanted to nip the problem in the bud. Oblivion King ruined your dad's plans by bringing you all to this world. What better way to get back at the one who sealed him away long ago than to destroy his children in front of him? Not only would the monster have his revenge, but there would be no one else in either world able to stop him. But, the king did not only want to destroy you because of your dad, your mom is 'special' too. She comes from a group of islands at the very heart of your Pacific Ocean. But hers is a story for later. Did you not wonder how we came to know how to create so many of your native dishes, or how the king of Heaven's Mirror came to know that you did not like to eat under water? The one you have come to call

Stormy, your dad, has been watching over you this whole time."

Celest was shocked, but deep inside she felt like she knew the entire time. Behind her John had been slapped from the sky, Eric was pinned underneath one of Oblivion King's clawed feet, and both Alex and Desmond were now laying unconscious on the hard earth. Something was triggered within Celest. She had rediscovered her dad only to watch him hover on the edge of death. The wind around her began to spin and intensify. Her hair was being blown across her face as she looked up at Oblivion King and snarled. "I have had more than enough of you!"

Celest walked toward the dark king. With every step the already dark night became darker still. Celest had her hands cupped to her right side. Soon with each of her steps the earth in front of her spiked up into pillars forming a rocky stairway. Each of her steps looked as if she was going to step right off of the pillar and plummet to her death, but each time the next stone pillar would spike up just in time to catch her foot and push her higher still. By the time she was level with the Oblivion King's face, the world around them was pitch black. The only one who could be seen was Celest. She could be seen because of the faint light coming from her cupped hands.

A booming voice came to her from the darkness that was the dark king's head, "This is your plan, to scare me with darkness? Fool I *am* darkness. You have only made me stronger!"

Celest gave a mirthless laugh, "You know what just occurred to me down there? Light, is an element too!"

She held her cupped hands toward the Oblivion King's face and opened them. A giant ball of light floated out and began peeling away all of the dark king's darkness, all of his dark powers. For a moment the form of Iron Back's cousin could be seen, it had the trace of a smile on its face before it crumbled to the ground. He was free at last. The enchanted night that ruled over the land was shattered and the first rays of sunrise warmed the weary group. Celest jumped down and ran to Stormy's side. He got up looking tired but alright. Terra and Oscar had used up six cans of lightning leaf paste to help him recover.

Celest threw her arms around Stormy's neck, and as she was holding him, he became a man. He had exotic features and fair skin that had a golden glow about it. John and Eric ran over to Stormy surprised by the change. Celest's eyes were full of happy tears as she hugged her dad and looked over his shoulder. Stormy held his daughter tightly and said, "I am really sorry that I never let you know who I was. I just did not want to frighten you away. But still, I am sorrier that I missed so much of your childhood." Celest began to sob at finally knowing why her dad was never around. Suddenly she saw her younger self standing in the distance smiling. The little girl waved and walked away. As she did so she faded into thin air. The little girl's voice filled her head one last time, "Never forget where you came from. Once you consciously know."

FAREWELLS

Oscar looked depressed as he said, "We can get you home now, anytime you like. But please, let us have a good-bye party in your honor first." Moments later Iron Back landed beside them. Other than a few deep cuts he seemed alright.

He looked at the Windhearts and said, "Well done! I expected nothing less."

As they left the castle, Celest could not help but smile at the restored forest. It was lush and green. Before the group could continue on, a beautiful woman and a gentle faced man appeared before them and smiled before disappearing in a gust of wind littered with orange blossoms. It was Princess Elena and Prince Bryan saying thanks before finally laying down to rest, their curse broken at last. Behind them they could hear mournful howling. They all turned around to see an old man standing in the middle of a large group of wolves. He grinned, turned, became a gray wolf and led his pack back into the depths of the forest.

A couple of days later they threw a grand party. Every creature they had met on their journey had attended, and along with them hundreds that they had not. Once the celebration grounds were full, Terra walked up onto a podium of sorts. At once the entire assembly fell into a deep silence to listen to her. She smiled at all of them, "You are all here to pay your thanks to the Windhearts for liberating our world from the clutches of Oblivion King. It is funny to me, a while ago Celest told me that this was like a world of fairy tales come to life for her. Little did she know that the greatest of *our* legends would come from hers, the magnificent legend of the Windhearts! To the Windhearts and their heroic spirit unyielding!"

The great assembly toasted the Windhearts at once in a single deafening voice, "To the Windhearts!"

The party was in full force when Oscar came up to the Windhearts' table, "I would like for you to come to my wedding. Preparations are already underway, and we will wait for your return to have the ceremony. I recently found out that Marlene feels the same way for me that I always have for her. She is to be my queen. Old friend would you be my, umm, best man?" Stormy smiled, he had once again become a winged storm steed, and nodded. Everyone but Celest and Alex began applauding Oscar's soon-to-be wedding. The reason that Celest and Alex did not join everyone else is that they were off together enjoying the music and dancing. The party lasted for three days straight. When people got tired they simply went into a nearby tent and went to sleep. When at last the party was finished, Oscar informed the Windhearts that it was time to go.

They took them to the place where Celest first entered the world that they had spent so much time maturing in. Celest asked sadly, "But how can we get back?"

Oscar smiled warmly. "Those charms I gave you can open any portal into this world. Just hold them up to a time piece of some sort and run the charm along its edge. Stormy would like you to give this pendant to your mom so that she can come and see him as well."

In the near distance Celest could see Stormy watching them, his eyes shimmering with raw emotion. Oscar then handed Celest a golden necklace with a diamond centerpiece surrounded with tiny multicolored pearls that made up the same fairy words that adorned the charms given to the Windheart children. Everyone hugged everyone goodbye, but Alex hung back. Celest looked up at him waiting for him to say good bye, but he never did. He instead began to walk away. Celest was just about to let him know how rude he was being by having a couple small rocks pelt him when Alex called over his shoulder, "Come back soon. I'll miss you." It was just then that Celest realized Alex was not trying to be rude. He just had a problem with goodbyes.

After Oscar had opened the portal, a dark howling filled the air, "I need a new body. Your mother's will do nicely!" Seconds later dark shadow made its way toward the portal. Stormy galloped at full speed toward the dark presence, his heart full of fear and anger. Even more than these two feelings, his heart was overcome with an unstoppable desire to protect those he loves and cherishes with his whole being. Celest seemed to feel her dad's feelings, and as they added themselves to her own, a raging thundercloud engulfed her. Flashes of lightning showed glimpses of a winged unicorn standing at the cloud's center. Suddenly a powerful blast of wind ripped the shadow from the ground, shredded it, and cast it into the distant mountains. After the essence of the dark king was no longer a threat, the storm faded and Celest returned to her normal state.

Oscar looked from the mountains to Celest, "I now believe you have your answer to the question about form changing. You *are* a storm by your own right, and you have everything you need inside. What you just showed us was a glimpse of your inner power, and how the love of your family brings out your true potential." Still a little shaken, Celest and her brothers all hugged Stormy one last time before jumping into the portal.

They soon found them selves back in Golden River's detention hall. It was late at night so they all left the school and headed home. When they got inside, they knocked on the door to their mom's room. Mrs. Windheart threw the door open and hugged her daughter and sons, who are human in our world. At least until they learn how to control their transformation as the great Stormy once did. John's regular eyesight was gone now that he was just a boy again. But like his siblings he kept his powers. So he could see his mother in other ways, and she was as beautiful as he always imagined her to be. Their mom told them that they had been gone for weeks, but the children felt like they had been gone for years. Celest gave her mom the gift that was sent there with her, and told her about all the time she had spent with her dad.

The children finished the school year and did a wonderful job at catching up with the other students. The bully who had hit John with the rock tried to pick on him again. When this happened John "looked" at him for a moment and said, "Maybe you should leave me alone, or I could tell everyone how you still wet the bed sometimes." The bully turned red and ran off.

At the end of the school year Celest and her family went into the living room. She walked up to the grandfather clock and used her ring to turn it into a portal. As they tumbled down the tunnel of light, John could feel his body growing smaller and his regular eye sight (well... regular for a golden eagle) return to him. Once they had landed they looked around for Mrs. Windheart. Instead of her thick black hair that fell to her mid-back, she had a mane that was whiter than the snow, and instead of her eyes being dark brown they were a silver gray. Their mother was now a dazzling white unicorn.

They could see Stormy flying in from the distance. Mrs. Windheart galloped up to meet him, the light in the air forming itself into a bridge beneath her hooves. The light would cradle her steps wherever she wanted to take them, and as unicorns do not grow tired she could easily follow Stormy anywhere she desired. Stormy led her to Rose Brew where their children had felt so much at home. Celest and her brothers took their mom to the fountain that the people of the town had put up in their honor.

John laughed and said, "When we came to this world we found out that a huge part of us was here the whole time, waiting for us. Not only our powers were awakened here, but we found our dad!"

Epilogue

Stormy and Mrs. Windheart do have real names, other than Dad, "Stormy," Mom, and Mrs. Windheart. But, Stormy and Mrs. Windheart is how *I* have come to know them. Perhaps I'll share their true names with you in another story at another time. Along with any other details I have neglected to share with you. Like how John and Eric finally mastered their abilities to control their transformations, and how Celest and Alex ended up together. Plus the joyous moment when John discovered that while he was human in "that other place" he could see. John was able to use his magnificent "sight" to become a sword master with no equal. In fact, the only ones able to even keep up with him when it came to swordsmanship were Oscar, Alex, and of course, Celest. Eric became a renowned hand to hand warrior. When he was old enough, Eric was trained by Terra and Desmond. He became the ultimate kick boxer, due to his super strength and agility. The Windhearts continued to be key protectors in both worlds. At the end of each school year, the Windheart family would meet at the grandfather clock in order to embark on another incredible journey. There are many important battles for you to read about in future additions to the story I have been telling you. As you now know, Oblivion King had been stopped cold, but for how long? This and much more is waiting for you to discover. Until the next time...

To my reader,

If I did a half-way decent job of telling you the Windhearts' story, then perhaps you are wondering what happened to them next. Well, I can assure you that their lives remained very interesting. In fact, sometimes more interesting than they would have liked. Their journeys through life reached legendary status. I hope that your own journeys are as rewarding and fulfilling as theirs. Maybe, if you have the time, I can tell you the rest of their story and perhaps the stories of other heroes. Until the next time I am *so* privileged to write you again, peace be *your* journey.

Thanks again,

Elvis Ray